TALES FOR MY GREAT-GRANDDAUGHTER

Tales for my Great-Granddaughter

Trevor Woolston

SERENDIPITY

First Published in 2004 by
Serendipity
Suite 530
37 Store Street
Bloomsbury
London

British Library Cataloguing-in-Publication data
A catalogue record for this book is available from the British Library
ISBN 1-84394-107-4

Printed and bound by Antony Rowe Ltd, Eastbourne

Contents

Foreword xi
The Cuckoo Clock 1
Secrets of the Apple Orchard 5
Growing Up 10
Games We Used To Play 15
Maggie York 18
Fishing 21
A Very Short Horror Story 23
The Corset Factory 25
The Premier Tailor 27
Intermission 29
Music – A Lifetime's Obsession 30
A. J., A Teacher to Remember 37
Uncle Harry 40
A Day Out with the Family 42
The Butcher's 48
Dr Gerald 50
Sunday School Anniversaries 52
The Hospital Fête 55
Collecting the Rents 59
A Bike Ride 63
The Arrival of the Cinema 68
Father's Family 72
Rowell Fair 77
Guy Fawkes 81
Grandad Dawkins Begins a New Life 84
Postlude 89

Acknowledgements

My deepest thanks to my wife, Emma, for her help and criticism. Andrew Payne, without whose computer skills this book might still be languishing in long-hand.

Belinda Humfrey, a reliable and firm link with my home town of Desborough. She is Chair of Desborough Civic Society which runs the Desborough Heritage Centre.

John Lee of the Desborough Heritage Centre.

Samuli Woolston, our grandson,
Finnish architect and designer, for his cover design and line drawings.

Dedication

To my great grandaughter, Jodie

Introduction

Childhood recollections are almost always attractive; but how charming are these descriptions of a boy's everyday life in the 1920s, simple, bounded, yet delightfully happy, exciting and creative for him. Trevor Woolston speaks of the 'near Victorian culture' he was born into in 1917 and his wish for continuity as he takes his newly-born great-granddaughter into the characterful life of the Victorian grandparents who brought him up (his father having been killed in 1918 in the War). We see the boy's life being formed by grandparents, mother, uncles, aunts and teachers. Yet readers of these 'Tales' from intermediate generations will enjoy his conjuring-up of a life which certainly continued into the 1950s in a majority of English families. Some of the anecdotal background, such as the 1926 General Strike, is dated. Street gas lamp-lighters, bedroom candles, the local doctor's operations on his patient's kitchen table, the silent cinema's pianist, the slaughter of animals in the butcher's yard, such as we meet incidentally in this book, were replaced by supposedly safer devices by the 50s, as cars and newly arrived television changed social life. (And I would hope attitudes have changed; here animal slaughter at the butcher's and in the harvest field is remembered as 'exciting' for boys - though a heifer's killing itself by the chains of a children's swing is accepted as sad.) However, the warmth of the family gatherings, the ingenuity of children's street and parlour games (though were 'Tit-tat-toe' and 'Puck-a-duff' universal?), the family enjoyment of day walks in the surrounding countryside, and a 'tight-knit community' continued for half-a-century – and in Desborough, even now, certainly the community.

Trevor Woolston recreates for us a boy's life in a special small town, Desborough in Northamptonshire, a town then of 4,000 population, now of 8,500 (though, within a few year's time, with the imposition of housing development, to reach 12,000). It is surprising how confined in space are this boy's adventures, mainly to the south-east of the town. Perhaps this is fortunate. The long High Street down which his grandfather marched with the cuckoo clock for repair (in the first story) together with Buckwell Street, which he regrets he visited disobediently (A Horror Story) was demolished for 1970s 'progress'. Substantial 17th and 18th century houses and cottages, three farms, twenty-two shops and three pubs, the majority of these buildings in local iron sandstone – which would have made Desborough a tourist attraction now – were swept away for a road-widening which was then abandoned. But this boy's rich life centres upon redbrick Desborough, the shopping street Station Road, running between the High Street and the railway station (opened 1857, closed in the 1960s) and the 1890s mainly terraced roads beyond the station. These roads are there now, with noticeably his grandparents' detached 4 Regent Street, only a few metres from the Pipewell Road railway bridge, the boundary of the infant's world. (His walk across its hump as a three-year old calls to mind the Northamptonshire poet, John Clare's infant walk attempt to reach the horizon.)

The railway bridge is the entrance to the then fascinating world of iron-ore quarrying, the engines and especially the plank across a gully, the 'Shaky Bridge' of beloved Desborough memory, the green fields of the Plens, now the name of an ironstone gully Nature Reserve (which is about to face the onslaught of housing estates all around it) and those long family walks, full of wild-life observation, to the Welland Valley. Down Regent Street in the opposite direction, Desborians can reach the 'Rec' of these stories and, continuing through post-War housing roads, can still reach the Ise Brook where the boy Trevor fished. Other buildings remain: the old Baptist Church became a Music Hall and is now a community centre; 0ddfellows which he saw become a cinema is still the Ritz, but is now used for dinners and dances; the fine Congregational Church in Paddock Lane of 1860 was replaced; the Corset Factory makes swimsuits; and the allotments at the top of Pioneer Avenue, the place of his grandfather's second apple orchard, have yet to be built upon.

This is a story of a bright boy with outstanding musical talent. The talent is nurtured not only by a special teacher but by his grandfather, a cellist and church- organist, and an aunt, a piano teacher. He wins one of the few places at Kettering Grammar School, seven miles away, and as a youth aspires successfully to own a car, a scarcity. But his stories are also confined socially, which dates them and adds extra interest. (Each story is like an old photograph in that it reveals more than the central focus.) His family are tradespeople, the Dawkins side are builders, prosperous, investing in property etc., but enjoy sidelines such as (sensibly) selling their apples. The family includes piano teachers, cobblers, skilled factory works ('clickers'); their womenfolk, even perhaps working briefly at the corset factory, having to work hard on washing day. In the Tales this family, complete in itself, lives very much in the present. Desborough has a proven long history, from royal Bronze Age and Anglo-Saxon remains – with Roman evidence in between. The young Woolston seems largely unaware of history. He does have passing thoughts of the Gunpowder Plot and the Civil War, though he puts the Plot in nearby Rothwell, despite the eminent Roman Catholic Pulton family in Desborough, and he is unaware that Cromwellians camped at Rothwell while Royalists were in the Church at Desborough before the Battle of Naseby. His mind is always on the violin he is to inherit from his uncle, the other family victim of World War I.

Desborough, having changed from a silk and silk-plush manufacturing town in the 1860s to boot and shoe making, had eleven shoe factories, of varying sizes, in the 1920s. In the Tales, the clickers, whom boys watched through factory windows, and in Maggie York's sweet shop, worked at the famous Cheaney's, and the dashing young man, the boss's son whose arrival in his sports car interrupts the boys' marble-playing in Regent Street, I know to be J. H. (Dick) Cheaney, who carried on that business brilliantly and, having only this year given up driving, is very much alive and only seven years older than TW. But how distant he is to the boys! I suspect that my other relatives of a couple of generations back, the Riley ancestor employing hundreds at the shoe factory where TW's grandfather worked, and the Humfrey owning a farm, were among those the young boy Trevor Woolston saw as 'toffs' - if 'toffs' had the advantages of governesses, longer schooling than most, horses, carriages, cars, chauffeurs, maids, etc. to make their lives smoother.

Yet how many small towns put on a polo match such as TW describes at their Carnival (The Hospital Fete)? Isn't polo a game for toffs? Was this only an event because fine polo ponies and hunters (bought by King George V) were bred by the Sumners of Desborough (whose own brightest horseman son was killed in World War I, like many Desborough men)? Young TW makes a passing reference to the point-to-point horse races at nearby Dingley; but the only real horse in his Tales is the milkman's. Yet the Rileys, Humfreys and Sumners were strongly supportive of the Congregational Church, that independent, middle-class, educational, democratic church which, the signs are, was at the centre of the strong family life of this boy. I would suggest that that church provided more for Desborough's 'tight-knit community' even in the 20s and early 30s than the orchestra and the amusing dramatic productions which the youth enjoyed via its Young Men's Bible Class.

We see in this book the enclosed world of a distinctive child's vision, and almost accidentally the characters and occupations and society of this town. Yet this innocent golden world is realistically conveyed; it is not the romanticised recollecting of John Clare or Dylan Thomas; there is a den in the coal cellar as well as in the apple tree. Desborians and their children will recognise their town here, and many of them will remember the people and places Trevor Woolston so vividly records. Indeed, some of the characters, in addition to the scenes, can be found in the extraordinarily rich photographic archives and displays in 'Desborough Heritage', the heritage centre recently set up by Desborough Civic Society.

Belinda Humfrey
Beeches House
Desborough

Foreword

It struck me, the other day, watching you in your play-pen, kicking your heels in the air and gurgling happily, how different little girls and little boys are. There is a certain contentment, an all-round observance of what goes on in that big, wide world you are beginning to discover. What was my childhood like, by comparison? Was it so different from yours that you would rather not know about it? Or would you be interested and intrigued by the background your great-grandfather came from? That sounds terribly, terribly old to call me a great-grandfather, but I still feel young, just like you. Maybe an older brother.

I decided to jot down a few simple stories of my childhood, about the near-Victorian culture I was born into and how the life of my parents and grandparents affected me, when I, too, was the youngest of the family. The same things were happening then as now, babies were being born, and growing up. Some old people, they seemed very old to me, even died. The First World War brought death to every door-step and vast changes followed. Now, the pace of change quickens. Life has become so dangerous, it frightens me to think how you will cope with it.

You, fortunately, do not know about those worries yet. So let me tell you some stories, happy stories, remembered by one small boy, me, from those comparatively peaceful times. Later on, you will have different, just as exciting stories to tell. Meantime, I hope you will love these, the essence of my childhood.

My father (Arthur Woolston) in uniform with his wife, my mother (Evelyn) and my brother Arthur (Artie). Father's last visit home on leave, November 1917 (before I was born.)

Mother in the orchard.

The Woolston family: *back row* Ernest, Arthur, Walter, Jack. *To the side* Mabel (*left*), and Clara (*right*). *Seated* Mary Jane (known as Poll), Grandma, Grandad, Em. *Foreground* Maud (*left*) and Hilda (*right*).

The Cuckoo Clock

It all happened a very long time ago, before I was born. Your parents would find it difficult to picture life then. To you, it will sound like a fairy story.

4 Regent Street was my grandparents' new home; built by Dawkins the Builders, who had already built most of Desborough, as it expanded with the growth of the boot and shoe industry, in the late Victorian era. Grandad Dawkins was one of the sons involved in the business. It was only to be expected that a valuable clock would grace a better-class home like his.

The Cuckoo Clock was a wedding present to my grandparents and they had given it pride of place near the open fire in the living room. It rested, confidently, on top of a cupboard full of wedding treasures. From the Black Forest in Germany, an area of highly-skilled clock-makers, wood-carvers and instrument-makers, the clock was one of the most impressive of its kind.

When I was old enough to stand and look at it carefully, the cuckoo would pop out, cheekily, telling me the exact time and demanding my full attention. I grew more attached to the clock, daily. Even though Grandad showed me some of its complicated mechanisms, how it regulated the time and ensured accurate striking on the hour and every half-hour, for me the clock was alive, a friend of mine. I used to stand and watch its face, its changing expression as the hands moved round. If I did not keep my eyes glued on it, I might miss that magic moment when it began the first strike, beginning with an internal whirr of machinery and then the clanging of a metal spring hidden by the clock's back door. Out popped the cuckoo, opening its mouth and closing it each time it announced the hour and then, just as quickly, darting back inside and closing the small door, just under the roof, where it first appeared.

After this sudden excitement, the clock face now showed how peaceful it could be, how skilfully it was constructed. A circular ribbon of ebony, with up to 12 white Roman numerals, showed the simple essentials of an hour. Each numeral was neatly fixed with a tiny nail. The ivory hands ingeniously mounted on a central axle, the minute hand outer-most and able to pass the smaller hour hand underneath. Inside the outer circle of ebony ribbon, carved wooden circles with key-holes, bored and containing metal sockets, one for the main clock mechanism and the other for the cuckoo and strike mechanism. Protruding from the side of the face, some carefully-carved lattice woodwork, giving the appearance of a miniature organ-loft, finished like a small piece of baroque art.

Since the arrival of the Cuckoo Clock, the Dawkins family had grown. There were now two daughters, my mother and Doris, my brother Arthur and me. My grandparents had a younger son, also Arthur, who had been killed in the First World War, along with my own father, another older Arthur, who met his death in the Spring of 1918 near Ypres. I had been born the previous December, but Father had never managed to come home on leave to see me. His letters spoke of that being his deepest wish in that merciless war. Mother, I was told, was distraught at this double loss and didn't speak for six months. It was hard to understand how she managed to bring up a very young baby and shower all her love on Arthur and me. But we were already a tightly-knit family, facing life's problems together, everybody taking care of each other.

There was another daughter, Elsie, older than Mother and Doris. She was the first to marry and, at first, lived in Rowell (my father's home town). Now Mother had moved to 4 Regent Street, it seemed sensible for Elsie and Fred Rains and their son, Howard, to move down to 17 Queen Street. That extended our family circle still more. Elsie was able to visit her parents daily and Arthur gained a playmate in Howard, a year younger than him.

The Cuckoo Clock remained my very own playmate, although a centre of attraction to every visitor. It seemed likely to stay that way for many years. But then, the wireless forced its way onto the small cupboard, standing alongside the Cuckoo Clock. A powerful, 3-valve set with a large HMV wooden horn, a mysterious newcomer and a little threatening to the Cuckoo Clock.

Soon after, the Cuckoo Clock stopped and, for all Grandad's coaxing, refused to start again. Grandad was getting upset. He had wound up the clock as usual and now took off the back to check inside. Nothing wrong with the springs, the clock's driving force, nor with the small cog-wheels, which kept the hands turning. The bellows provided wind and notes for the cuckoo and the vertical wooden strut was intact, which enabled the cuckoo to bow out of its door and open and close its mouth for each 'Cuckoo!' Grandad had to concede that it was a job for the expert, the local clock-repairer.

The town's clock-maker and repairer was, surprisingly, a German. Possibly a prisoner-of-war, he had married a Desborough girl and chose, gladly, to live in this out-of-the-way town, where he could follow his old profession and come to be regarded as an invaluable newcomer. The boot and shoe factories started at 7:30 every morning, so clocks were needed to make sure the workers got there in time to start work. Any worker 'clocking on' late lost 'a quarter' from his hourly pay. At the back of all this bustle, the quiet work of the clock-maker was a god-send and he could be relied on to carry out repairs in double quick time.

It was said that the Desborough expert had an even greater responsibility back in Germany, where every town-hall boasted a special clock belfry. Imposing painted wooden figures were made to move in and out of their home at the top

Grandad and Grandma in the orchard.

of the tower. Visitors to the town gathered below to admire their stately antics. The clock-maker had been responsible for one such belfry, but was said now to prefer smaller, more delicate work on clocks.

Grandfather covered the Cuckoo Clock with a blanket and set off with it in his arms down Station Road then turned left towards the clock-maker's workshop in the High Street. He had to pass the Co-op grocers, the butcher's, the baker's and the chemist's so he was bound to attract a lot of attention. Grandad did not stop but swiftly passed the Post Office and the old Stone Cross seeking to reach the shop he wanted as soon as possible. At this point, to the surprise of everybody within earshot, the cuckoo began to strike. There was no hiding it. It just went on and on and on! All very reasonable, I thought. The cuckoo was objecting strongly to being taken blind-fold into unfamiliar territory – maybe abroad – back to the Black Forest! Grandfather, very embarrassed, speeded up, set the clock down on the shop counter and whipped the blanket off. The Cuckoo stopped immediately. Grandad sighing with relief, explained his mission to the smiling German, who appeared from the back, keen as ever to help. After a brief examination, it was agreed the clock should stay for a holiday and enjoy a general check-up. Maybe the clock had been working too hard lately.

Grandfather made his way back up the High Street, relieved but a bit sad to lose his daily companion. Naturally, a lot of his friends stopped him to ask what was wrong with the Cuckoo Clock, whom they knew well. Some commiserated, others tried to cheer Grandad up, promising the clock would soon be back home. One wag started to hum a favourite tune of the day 'The Grandfather Clock' and then to sing

90 years without slumbering
Tick, tock; tick tock
Life's seconds numbering
Tick, tock; tick tock
It stopped! Short! Never to go
again ...

The singer stopped abruptly, remembering the last line ended with 'when the old man died', fearing such a suggestion might cause offence. A mutual exchange of jokes followed and Grandad went home to break the news that the Cuckoo Clock had been left behind, for a holiday.

Grandma and I at the seaside.

Grandad died many years later and the Cuckoo Clock came to live with me. I wind him up twice daily, before I go to bed and again, first thing in the morning. It's remarkable how the cuckoo perks up when he gets that kick-start every morning. Just like he used to, if I forget the cuckoo stops accusingly half-way out of his door, mouth open, out of breath and very upset. Not to be taken lightly by me, who should know better than to forget life's essentials. 'Don't forget to wind the clock, night and morning!' I can hear Grandad say.

When you are a bit older, Jodie, and you sense the excitement generated by our Cuckoo Clock, he may well become your daily companion. He would love to see more children around, waiting for him to strike. It would almost be a replay of the scene in No. 4 Regent Street. That would help all of us to feel young again.

Secrets of the Apple Orchard

One of the glories of my grandparents' house was its garden. Visitors coming through the side-gate would be surprised to find a large orchard had been hidden by the houses all round. Most of it stretched along the back of a row of red-brick houses, built in a continuous terrace. They had been for the railway workers, at a time when railways were expanding, and stood on Station Road, facing the extensive goods-yard, which adjoined the Station itself. Originally, they were in pairs to a regular pattern, with one house facing another at the back and access provided through a common entry. Gates to the right and left then gave some privacy to conversations at the back doors. When the terrace was sold off, at a time when there were fewer railway workers, the new owners soon began to make changes. The regular style of the original buildings might now have bay windows and new doors added at the front. At the back, extra small buildings appeared, some for storage but others, in wood, with hen runs. Local people felt the need for fresh eggs daily for growing families. They had been used to their own vegetables, if they had come from country small-holdings.

The garden of the last of the terraced houses came down to our top corner, where a huge cherry tree, a white-heart, was growing. It was an impressive feature, placed so neatly there, but the disadvantage for me was its enormous bottom trunk. You needed a ladder even to get started and climb higher up, where the bunches of cherries grew.

The garden turned the corner there. Another row of small houses in Queen Street had gardens, which, like the ones up to the corner, stretched down to the orchard and formed another boundary. The third side was the full length of the garden of No. 6 Regent Street, the neighbours we had most to do with. Anybody standing in one of the gardens on our perimeter could come to the end and look over to see what was going on. After all, on most days, there would be some activity, even if we were only picking up fallen apples.

The fences all round did not necessarily stop us squeezing through gaps. Our neighbours had, sometimes, to climb over to recover a hen which had got out. To maintain contact with Elsie, Grandad's eldest daughter and her family, Grandad, with some help, had laid a blue stone slab path to the end of Elsie's garden, where a gate ensured nobody else claimed a right of way.

The whole of this roughly triangular area was covered with fruit trees, mainly apples. They had been planted over several years and that helped to produce both small and large trees, with pear trees topping the rest. Grandad used a short ladder, made by him, of course, to pick apples within reach. He could reach some of the higher ones, by using the crook of his walking-stick to pull them towards his other hand. I knew all the wonderful names given to each variety – Newton Wonder, Prince Albert, Coster, Bramley and Cox. Cox had a special place near my aunt's garden and produced small, sweet red and brown apples, totally unlike the large standard varieties of today, and to my recollection, far better in taste. The pear trees, tall and straight, provided a wonderful view if you could manage to climb to the very top. Williams, Conference, Hazel and my favourite, a very special Green Pear, which always went by that name. These were stewing pears, too, quite unlike the rest, which never seemed to get ripe. When they, at last, started to drop to the ground, we picked them up in a basket and took them to Grandma to stew, with custard. No red wine in those days. Only home-made, sweet white wine, made from elderflower or cowslips, which carpeted the woods nearby.

The orchard was that wonderful, spacious hide-away place where we could easily get lost. As the top of the garden, on the way to Aunt Elsie's, there was a luscious Victoria Plum, growing on a high brick wall. We could really taste the juice as we bit into them and extracted the stone. The wasps would, sometimes, get there first. Near that plum tree, Grandad had a series of old buildings, formerly big sties in which he kept his beautifully painted green wheel-barrow and a much heavier, rough and ready truck. He had mackled this together, with two heavy metal wheels and two legs to support it. Two wooden handles fixed to the loading box of the truck were used to lift it, and when setting off for the allotment, it was certainly much too heavy for Grandad, especially when fully loaded.

In these sheds, too, were a great many tools for gardening and building work, which I could borrow, when I fancied some digging. Nearer the house, was an old damson tree, which I soon found treacherous to climb. Its branches broke without warning and landed me on the ground, too near a glass greenhouse for comfort.

Nearer still to the house, was a carefully hidden outside toilet. No running water there. We had to flush it with buckets of water, carried down from the house. Next to it, the all-important wash-house. On Mondays, Grandma and Mam would be busy there at an early hour, preparing for the weekly washday. Even before them, Grandad had filled the copper with water and started a fire under it. The fuel was mostly sacks of off-cuts of leather, chips they were called, from the factory opposite. Very smoky, but producing plenty of heat.

The zinc dolly-tub was a central feature, standing on the floor with its 3-legged wooden plunger ready to attack the pile of dirty clothes and used, to twist to and fro, to remove all the dirt. The wet clothes then had to be put through the mangle several times, until its wooden rollers had squeezed all the water out. With sighs of relief from Grandma and Mam, the clothes were, finally, pegged on the line, which stretched from the back door of the house, halfway up the garden-path.

Monday was dedicated to the women of the house and they were in control. Children had to steer clear. We might venture back there, when Grandma went indoors to set the table for dinner. Monday's dinner was always cold meat, the remains of Sunday's roast joint. We had to fill up with lots of small potatoes, still in their skins and boiled in a large, brown pot.

Whilst all was quiet and everybody had gone indoors, I had a secret assignment, up a tall red cherry tree. This had grown outside the wash-house, but was now so tall that the top branches overlooked the yard next door. From this vantage point, I could take a peep at next door's beautiful baby, outside their back door and left to keep warm in the sunshine. She was a delight to watch and so happy and contented. Occasionally, she would wake up and yell for her Mam. I would then, discreetly, climb down, hoping I had not been seen, and disappear into the wash-house. I might be left to play there, until the clothes on the outside line had dried and Grandma and Mam began to take them indoors, ready to fold and iron on Tuesdays.

Tuesday was the day for shin of beef, boiled on the stove, in another brown pot and then put through a mincing machine, fixed to the edge of the table. This worked by turning a handle and so forcing the beef out in tiny pieces. Sometimes, I was allowed to turn this handle and make the minced meat come out into a dish, in which it would be cooked. There were interesting bits of meat compressed inside the mincer and a metal piece which had to be taken out and the meat removed. I was allowed to pick these small bits of meat out. It was surprising how much better they tasted than the rest compressed into the cooking bowl. The old kitchen range was now out of use and a gas stove had been squeezed into a small space at the top of the cellar steps. Certainly well out of the way, but, surely, very dangerous for Grandma to be lifting heavy and hot pots off the top to be set down in the kitchen.

The brick steps led down to another secret place, the cellar. This, after more steps, turned left and revealed a large, underground room, below the 'front room' where Doris kept her piano and all her music. I could listen to her playing or teaching a young pupil as I worked below, but I had to stay quiet. It was a magical place to hide in. One end window let in some light from the front of the house. It was a wooden structure, which was taken out when the coalman came to deliver a ton of his fuel. On the outside, in the front garden, was an iron grill, which could be lifted so that the coalman could tip his 1cwt sacks into the cellar. It was not easy to achieve this and he would have to come inside and shovel the loose coal to the outside wall. Some of it was in huge lumps, which had to be broken up later with a heavy hammer. The delivery stirred up a lot of coal dust and we had to take care to protect the apples stored on the opposite wall.

The apples had been stored on the basis of 'waste not, want not!' The basic idea was that there was a large wide wooden shelf on which the most prolific varieties were stored. Above this, smaller shelves for special but less plentiful varieties. Nearer the end steps, so that we could pick out any that were going bad, the heap of fallen apples we had brought in. Every shelf had to be covered by newspaper to give some protection against the coal dust.

When the time came for apples to be sold, Grandad would carefully select the best, weigh them on his solid steel scales – a balance with a variety of round iron weights on the other side from the apples – and then sort them into suitable containers, so the apples were not damaged and ready to sell. They cost mostly two pence a pound, but, the best attracted three pence. Fallen apples, which poorer families bought, were several pounds for a penny. Mostly, they were bought and sold by local shops, but there were callers who came for a few pounds, perhaps to make blackberry and apple jam.

There was a surprise in store for me, which adults had been secretly talking about amongst themselves. Grandad, as the one who dealt with the sale of apples, told me about the surprise the night before it happened. Mam had been a bit hesitant, imagining all kinds of accidents for me on the way. But Grandad insisted that it was a regular occurrence every year as it did nobody any harm. It was just the venture a boy would love to undertake. Besides, somebody had to take apples up to Rowell as it was much too far to carry them or even push them in his truck uphill.

On this very special day, after he had completed his morning round, the milkman arrived outside with his horse and cart, having left his milk churns and cans and measures behind at the farm. Everybody loaded the cart with some of our best apples. They were being taken to a shop in Rowell, 2 miles away, mainly uphill. The milkman sat at the front of the cart, reins in hand and found a reasonably comfortable place for me over the cart wheel. He made sure I would be aware of the dangers of falling over the side of the cart. Mam thought I should be tied in.

With a flick of the reins on the horse's back-side, we set off, through Desborough main street, past the church, down the hill past the Co-op Corset factory and we were soon in open country going down Bassett's Hill and over the Ise Brook. The descent was a bit scary, but to make sure the weight did not make it run away and crash, the milkman steered the cart into the stone edge of the footpath at the side of the road. Carts in those days had primitive brakes and it was sensible to let the steel bands round the wooden wheels rub against this stone kerb, which, effectively, slowed the cart down. The milkman teased me about this manoeuvre and suggested that we might let the cart go downhill freely so as to get rid of its cargo in the river. We wouldn't have to climb the hill ahead, in that case. Needless to say, he had done this trip many times before and was quite used to avoiding such hazards.

Soon, we were climbing up Rowell Hill, past Halfway House, a farm that marked the boundary between Desborough and Rowell. I could look back and see the church spire standing above the fields on the outskirts of the town and the footpath leading below the church to the river. On the other side of the main road were two avenues, rising to allotments on the outskirts opposite. On one of these avenues, my violin teacher lived. Rising so high and soon to reach Rowell, I could begin to feel superior on a journey that few of my friends had undertaken.

The road, at last, began to flatten out. At the top, we turned left past the Cricket Ground and the site of the old Abbey, or descended into the centre of the town. I had been told that an underground passage had been formed there, through which Guy Fawkes, when he was being sought by Protestant soldiers, could escape to the Catholic hide-out of the Treshams at Rushton Hall. But now, we were at the shop, welcomed by the lady in charge, who, immediately, invited me in and offered me sweets or something I fancied in the shop. Meantime, the milkman carried the boxes of apples in, had a friendly consultation with the lady about how many apples he had brought, collected the money and called to me:

'Come on, young fellow. We have got to get back home in time for tea!'

I got into the cart, an experienced hand. Phew! I breathed again, but it would not be so scary going back.

Growing Up

My aunts were all agreed, great aunts too of that I was an unusual child, just as you, undoubtedly, will be, but very different. Perhaps mischievous, up to unexpected tricks. Hiding under the living room table, appearing suddenly and even, it was said, chasing my youngest aunt round the table with a carving knife. No malice intended, I feel sure, simply aimed at livening up the evening, when great aunt's long and tedious tales seemed to be lasting all night. You might guess I was a Sagittarian.

At any rate, I grew up free and independent – a golden-haired child, whom everybody spoilt. At 3, I was told, I took off up the street, crossed the road at the top, where the ash tree grew, and was seen disappearing over the railway bridge to discover what the rest of the world had to offer. All sorts of exciting things to a child. Dangerous, according to the adults. My aunt saw me just disappearing over the hill, ran after me and dragged me back home, protesting wildly.

However, I had caught sight of steam locomotives through the criss-cross fence, intended to keep children off the railway line. Later on, I could go back with other boys to watch these engines racing down the straight piece of line past the allotments. It was a little bit frightening to watch these trains, pulled by powerful engines. They seemed to get bigger and more powerful the nearer they got. Most threatening when, with a great 'Whoosh …' they burst through the bridge and on to our station, speeding north. We could see even better by sitting on the embankment on the north side of the bridge, where we could wave to the engine driver and the fireman. The passengers, too, waved. We felt we had friends aboard.

At the top of this embankment, a static water-tank had been built on brick supports and a side line led to the tank, where engines involved in shunting trucks could fill up their water-tanks. We soon learnt that the engines needed water to make the steam, which drove the pistons connected to the iron wheels on the rails. The fireman was always busy shovelling coal into the fire-box below the engine's water-tank. But he had to watch what was ahead, as well as the driver, to make sure there was enough coal on board to get them to their destination.

The static water-tank was near the office of the Sheepbridge Iron and Steel Company, the company involved in digging out our ironstone from open-cast mines and leaving our fields almost like a wasteland of heaps of soil and rubble taken off the ironstone level. We didn't like our fields being ruined, but there were lots of new places where we could play.

We were careful to avoid being spotted, if anyone came out of the office to go to the pits. If we were spotted, we were quickly sent outside their property, back to the road. Our view was that there was a public footpath going past the office across to the Plens and we had a right to be there. It never occurred to us that they might think we would be safer well away from the railway-line. There was another separate side line on which trucks full of ironstone were pulled along on a continuous hefty wire, loaded at the pits and then taken to the goods yard for loading into railway trucks. These trucks then had to be connected and drawn by a goods engine to the smelting-mill.

Happy days, indeed, before I went to school. I still remember standing on a mat at the foot of the stairs and thinking, seriously, 'I am 4 now. I'm beginning to get grown up.' It was my birthday and the design of that hand-made mat is still as vivid to me as it was then.

The School was a central feature of the village. An Infants' Department with 4 to 7 year-olds and separate Senior girls and boys Departments, 8 to 14, separated and marking the enormous leap from children to budding adults. The separation was also emphasized by the enclosure of the Senior School in tall heavy iron railings and a gate with a lock on it. That, at any rate, ensured that irate parents, whose children had been punished in a way they disapproved of, were kept out of range of the threatened teacher.

The Infants' School, with a plump and loving headmistress in charge, seemed to us children very much like the extension of home, but following a regular system of periods devoted to teaching. We sat, two together, boy and girl, in tight wooden desks with iron supports, usually looking straight ahead at the teacher. Our first taste of learning the 3 Rs was to learn from coloured drawings on the wall. 'A is for apple.' 'B for bee.' 'C for cat.' I learned easily. In my case, I had learned to read at home. But my desk partner, a well-endowed young lady of my age named Ethel, had other ideas. Curiously, even at 4, she had formed the opinion that she should supplement my education with, to her, far more interesting facts of life. She soon started to guide my hand up her knickers, so that I could investigate what secrets were to be found there. Embarrassing but she was right, this was something new and interesting to a boy. In time, I was to learn there was a great deal more to this girl/boy relationship. Why did older boys and girls go off alone into the fields? Why did one of these older boys organize parties of boys to go with him and his young sister to a secret assignment down in the allotments?

Naturally, my interest in girls started to widen. There were other girls, rather more attractive than Ethel. One revealed herself to likely boys by running wildly about the asphalt playground and inviting them to chase her. A mop of curly

My first class in Senior School. (Top of my head at third desk back on the right).

hair added to her attractions and more might have come of this relationship, had we not been separated at 7 and moved up to our separate schools.

My first class in the all-boys school was taken by another motherly lady, who liked to get her favourites up front near her at her desk. There were opportunities here for a quick cuddle, but she could be just as fearsome dealing with anyone who misbehaved. After some weeks in that class, just when we were beginning to work together, the brighter ones doing what they could to help those in difficulty, a new boy appeared, unknown to any of us. He was strangely dressed to begin with, velvet collar on his jacket and hair standing up. It was our usual practice to spend the first period with the whole school gathered together in the hall (not so much a hall as two classrooms made into one and the partition between opened up) for prayers, led by the headmaster. He bore the rather Dickensian name of Grudgings, and lived up to it by picking out boys who didn't behave as he thought they should, and standing them in front of the school to be dealt with after prayers finished. Strangely, the new boy was excused going to prayers and left with our teacher to catch up on work he had missed early in that term. It turned out he was a Catholic. To us, surrounded by C of E Church and school, Baptist, Wesleyan and Congregational Church, meeting a Catholic was a strange experience. We were all probably somewhat relieved when he and his family moved elsewhere.

In those days, it was usual to move bright boys, who were not being stretched in the younger classes, fairly rapidly up the school. In this way, I soon experienced the vicissitudes of life with a teacher who specialized in throwing his short stick, with bulbous handle designed to be held, across the classroom. Unfailingly, it hit the offending miscreant who had not been paying proper attention, and the master would tell the boy to return the stick so that the lesson might continue.

Very soon, I arrived in the 'scholarship class', which had taken over the biggest room in the school. There the real delights began. The senior master, usually known as A. J., introduced us to the delights of Shakespeare and more especially Dickens with A. J. acting out the parts in front of us and thus ensuring we not only paid attention, but also absorbed the jewels of English literature. A. J. was also an outstanding violinist and had won a gold medal some years ago, when he passed, with honours, the examination for Fellowship of the College of Violinists, a College set up by leading British performers 'for violinists and run by violinists.' This was to be a huge influence on me from the age of 8 onwards, but more of that later.

I was evidently progressing rapidly to the top of the school and soon was in the top class, a 9 year-old mixed up with the 13/14 year-olds. The teacher of this top class was Mr Grudgings and the only respite we got from his intensive lessons was a double period spent in his garden, which adjoined the school. To begin with, it introduced us to hard work, digging the ground, removing weeds, bushes and undesirable growths and then learning how to produce worthwhile crops. It was our little patch, in which we could take some pride, and an area of learning I had already begun with my grandfather.

But being in the top class with older boys was not without its problems. The older, bigger boys, naturally, resented the introduction of a mere tich into their group, and on equal terms. They took every opportunity of getting their own back, often by lying in wait for me as I left school. I was, of course, out-numbered and had little chance of taking on the whole group, so I had to learn, as I already had with my older brother, to fight for my rights. I took on all and sundry with some vigour and was lucky, at times, to cause my opponent to retreat with a bloody nose. Soon, I got a reputation for being a young fighter not to be meddled with. It was the practice when one of these fights was in prospect to form a circle round the participants and cheer us on.

By the time I won a scholarship to the local Grammar School (then largely fee-paying) I was clearly one of the leaders of the new boys. We travelled daily by train, two stops down the line, taking about a quarter of an hour. The carriages sometimes had individual compartments and sometimes led off a long corridor. New boys settled for the journey in one of these corridor compartments, often found second-year boys roaming along the corridors, looking for newcomers to set on. Their favourite occupation and delight was in forcibly de-bagging their male victim and exposing him to the ridicule of passers-by. It was an effort to show how manly they were by comparison. The practice had spread to public schools and colleges and even universities, I learned later. Hardly the practice of grown-up men, not even for small boys who, mostly, knew better. But then …

Do you know what little boys are made of?
Slugs and snails and puppy-dog's tails.
That's what little boys are made of!

But then …

Do you know what little girls are made of?
Sugar and spice and all things nice.
That's what little girls are made of!

Games We Used To Play

As soon as I was able to lose my total dependence on Mother, I tagged on to groups of children, who, after school, were happily playing all kinds of mysterious games in our street. It was usually at dusk, when the lamp-lighter came round. Quickly and easily, he lit the street gas lamps, reaching up to the pilot light with a burning wick on the end of a long pole. Then he adjusted the flame to just the right level.

One of these lamps was placed on the bend in the road. Looking as permanent as a lighthouse, every night it lit up our bedroom, as well as the play area below. When we agreed, finally, to obey Mother's repeated demands to come in and get ready for bed, we could still watch the games going on. Eventually, all the children gave up and we had to deal with our own imagination, as mysterious shadows appeared to continue their own games on our bedroom. It was all a bit frightening and to counter these imagined threats, I would secretly call upon my own supporting group to keep guard over us, throughout the dark night, when our bedroom candles had been put out. There was I, in a double bed, my brother on the outside, the house wall protecting me on the other side. Later on, Mother, in another double bed in the other part of the room, provided all the protection we needed.

What were these mysterious games? The favourite with younger boys was marbles. Certainly a game of skill. First, a large coloured glass ball, known as the alley or boss, was thrown towards the foot of the street lamp. Usually, it ended in the gutter, an uneven, rough area. This established the area of play. The aim was then to get your smaller, brown marbles as close as possible to the 'alley'. A promising and accurate throw could still roll away, whilst a poor throw could, perversely, end by rolling closer.

These were free and happy days for children to play in the streets. I was later amazed to find that marbles in a great variety of versions was played throughout Europe, but we, naturally, assumed it was our special, secret game. Almost no traffic to interrupt us. No cars, at any rate. An occasional horse and cart or, more exciting, the arrival of the water-pump, a huge dray with the water-tank on top and pulled by a pair of horses. From this cylindrical tank, an open sack was lowered into the manhole above the sewer and water pumped through the sack to clean out the sewer below. The game had to stop and the braver boys gathered round the man-hole to watch what was happening below.

As time passed, there were more interruptions of our games. The son of the boot and shoe factory boss would come roaring down the street in his latest sports-car, with its open top and lots of gleaming brasswork. Certainly, a show stopper until he drove inside the factory and we could resume our game. The attraction of marbles was still, partly, that we could play safely in the dark. Some of the other games would be dangerous.

Conkers was not especially dangerous, just aggressive, but, again, played to strict rules. It was quite enough to play in a corner of the school playground, one-to-one between two boys with others watching to see who won. Prize conkers were chestnuts carefully collected under the huge trees which grew in the fields on the other side of the Ironstone Pits. When there was a shortage, a few hefty sticks thrown up at the tree would, usually, bring more chestnuts down. The conkers might then be baked in a hot oven and hardened. A hole was bored through them, so that the best could be put on strings. The boy who had first go took hold of his conker with one hand and aimed it with the other hand to hit his opponent's conker, hanging down loosely and vertically. If neither conker split, the other boy had his shot and so on until one or the other conker cracked and fell to the ground. Champion conkers (maybe, derived by name-shortening from 'conquerors') earned a great reputation and were followed around by supporters. Some claimed to have smashed 12 others and were known as twelvers. So the champion, for the time being, was followed around by cheer-leaders, as he set up to earn another victory. There was huge disappointment, if the champion fell at one blow from a mere newcomer.

An even more complicated game, which required plenty of space above and around, was called 'Tit-tat-toe.' Each player had a long ash-stick and a very short one, pointed at both ends. The game began with the small pointed stick placed across a hole. The long stick was then placed underneath it and the small stick slung sky-wards as high and far away as possible. The player then ran after it and hit its point to make it jump in the air. During its short flight, the pointed stick was struck hard and hit further away still. There was no telling where it might land. Maybe in our neighbour's front garden or the large Nursery, a favourite haunt of mine, whose gardens were full of vegetables and unknown flowers.

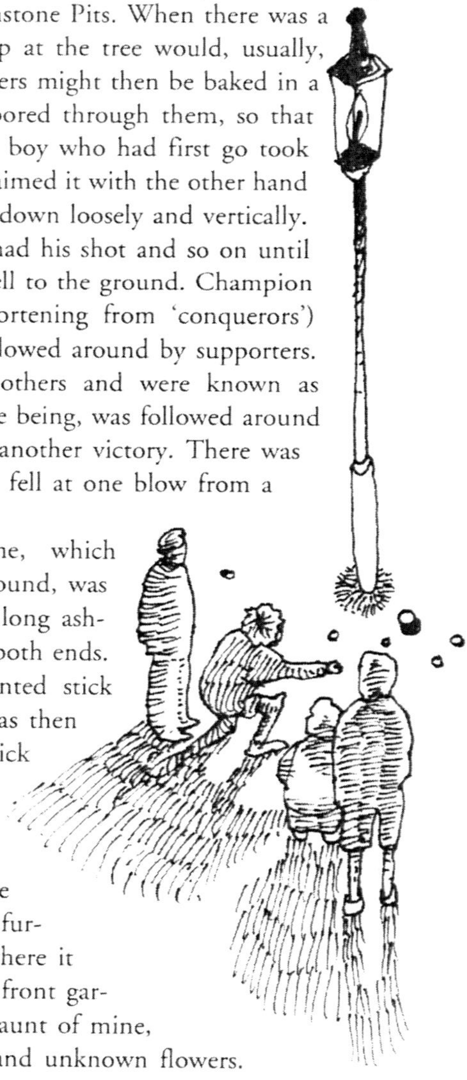

Windows were always in danger when this game was played. It was as well that spectators should not get too near. If the player who began missed an attempt to hit the small stick and it fell back on to the ground, another player could then take over and attempt to hit it back to the base where it all started.

A rougher game played by bigger boys and aspiring younger ones was called 'Puck-a-duff.' The biggest boys bent over with their hands and arms against a wooden door or tall gate, usually two side-by-side. Other boys leaned on these leaders, heads down and grasping the bodies in front. A third row formed up at the back, so that they all linked together, much like a rugby scrum. The opponents then formed up on the opposite side of the road and ran across, jumping on the backs of the bent figures. The aim was for the leaders to land as far forwards as possible with the rest swiftly following. With the attackers yelling 'Puck-a-Duff', the aim was to land with sufficient force to bring down the scrum. 'Puck-a-Duff' seemed to be some foreign war-cry!

All these games were mainly for boys. Girls kept well clear, playing quiet games like 'hide and seek', 'hop-scotch' and lots of skilled skipping games, which boys seemed to steer clear of. Boys' liking for more aggressive games did not disappear altogether as they got older. Tit-tat-toe re-appeared among grown men as 'Knur and Spell', using bigger sticks.

The most aggressive game seemed to come at the end of corn harvests. Farmers, with guns, their dogs held on a lead, arranged themselves on the four sides of the cornfield and waited for the corn-cutter, pulled by a horse, to start a job which could take all day. On the previous day, farm workers had scythed the whole of the cornfield's four sides in a band wide enough to allow the cutter to deal with the rest, each circuit slowly reducing the size of the inner square of corn.

The really exciting part, at least so far as the marksmen were concerned, was at the end of the day, when there was just a small square of corn left in which rabbits, an occasional hare and even a fox were hiding. Suddenly, the frightened animals broke cover and ran for the comparative safety of the hedgerows. The men with guns fired at close range and all the dogs had to do was to run and pick up the dead animals. The field was soon reduced to stubble, with the farmers smiling broadly and comparing how many dead animals each had acquired. At last, they went off home, leaving workers and their wives to stack sheaves of corn and to rake up any worthwhile leavings. On another day, the sheaves would be stacked on a haycart and taken to the mill for heads of corn to be extracted and ground. It seemed all too exhausting to those of us there simply to watch. But the tiredness was soon dissipated, when more women arrived with a substantial supper. Everybody was invited to join in and a great celebration followed, lasting after darkness had fallen. Maybe when the carts returned next day to clear the fields, we would get a ride on top of the sheaves.

Maggie York

A major figure in my young life was Maggie York. She ran a tiny shop just down the street from our house and opposite the factory. She was the unmarried daughter of Mr York, the nurseryman, whose greenhouses and plant-growing area extended between the shop and the next house to us. He grew all kinds of flowers, mostly those we couldn't easily get started, and supplied us with lettuces, peas and beans, celery and a few root crops. He was an important man, whom we learned to respect, but also a kind man, who let me play in his nursery, even to dig up plants I fancied and hoped to take home. If this happened, he would suggest we re-planted my prizes, but maybe take one of them home, with a flower on it, so that I could put it in my own small garden.

Mr York also kept bees and had a few hives hidden behind his greenhouses. We were expected to stay away from this area, in case the bees became angry at our intrusion. When the summer came, the bees left their hives and followed the queen, which usually made direct for our garden. Her preferred place to settle was the tall pear tree, the nearest fruit tree to the hive. When the whole swarm had settled there, we ran to tell Mr York. He soon appeared in full beekeeper's gear – a straw hat, covered by a veil, which hung down and protected his face. His arms and hands were uncovered. After all, he told us, the bees knew he was a friend and would never sting him.

By now, the swarm formed a large egg-shaped core. Slowly and carefully, Mr York placed a net below and with the aid of a smoke-puffer, which he squeezed from time to time, lured the whole colony into it. That done, he brought his barrow and a large basket-box designed to prevent the bees from escaping and rapidly wheeled his treasured bees back to where they belonged. This was probably in a fresh hive prepared for the bees to start a honeycomb. After a somewhat noisy protest about being taken away from that lovely pear blossom, the bees settled down quite happily.

I can picture Mr York taking off his net and straw hat and disappearing quietly behind his greenhouses. After a while, he would appear quite happy and unflustered and tell us we could go and tell Maggie the bees had settled in their new home and would soon begin to produce honey. She could think about getting the honey jars out, washed and ready for the shop.

It was all very exciting to me. Mr York was such a nice man, but Maggie was even nicer. Every customer in her shop, even one who could hardly reach the counter, was all important. I went there every week to spend my penny a week pocket money. There seemed to be an endless choice. Sweets of all kinds filled glass jars on the counter and on the shelves at the back. I had favourites like gob-stoppers – huge lumps of coloured balls I could scarcely get into my mouth. My mother was always afraid I would choke on them, but I reassured her, as I sucked, by taking the gob-stopper out and showing her how the colour had magically changed. There were plenty of alternatives – liquorice delights, aniseed balls, stickjaw toffee, and later on, chocolate. The chocolate, Maggie assured me, I would be able to try when I was bigger. After all, a bar of Cadbury's Bournville or Milk chocolate cost 2 pence. I didn't earn 2d until I was big enough to collect rents from a row of houses Grandad's firm had built in Queen Street. When I became responsible for collecting all that money – 1/2d a week for the smaller houses and 1/6d for the bigger ones – I suggested Grandma might like to pay me a bit more. My pocket money leapt to 6d a week, wealth indeed, which had to be spent carefully. If I spent 2d on a bar of chocolate it usually had to be cut in half, so that my brother, Arthur, could share it.

The great attraction of Maggie's shop was the bell, which rang as I opened the door to go in. It was necessary to alert Maggie that she had a customer in the shop, but it was usually better for me to go at less busy times, so that full attention could be given to the spending of my penny or two pence. If I happened to go in when the men at the factory opposite were having a short break, they would come pouring across the road and set the bell ringing time and again. The one pleasant ring that I produced was changed into a constant rhythm of interruptions. There was nothing for it but to take my bag of sweets and disappear. There were then so many men crowded into the shop, joking, and sometimes trying to talk to me, that I had to wait some minutes before I could leave. I was amazed by the variety of sweets, cakes and cigarettes that Maggie sorted out and handed over in double quick time. The men had need to be back at work on time and could not be given the same attention as was given to me.

As a result of those encounters, some of the clickers working at the windows overlooking the street used to wave to me. I was able to see how quickly and skilfully they trimmed the edges of the uppers with sharp knives and assembled them to be finished later into boots and shoes. One of these clickers was my Uncle Fred, who was married to Auntie Elsie, the Dawkins' eldest daughter. He could, no doubt, tell the others who I was and so very soon all the men would pause and wave, when they saw me passing by.

There was one incident which sticks in my memory and which illustrates Maggie's care and attention. I had somehow got hold of a silver coin – either a florin or half-a-crown, which the family liked to keep for a while, when they were issued brand new from the Mint – and took it down to Maggie's to find out what it would buy. I could not have been very old, since I put the coin almost above my head on the counter.

Maggie picked up the coin and asked me where I got it from. Probably, I said I had found it or else Mother or Grandma had given it to me.

Maggie said it was a very nice coin to have, but it wasn't the right one to buy sweets. She suggested I should take it home and ask Grandma to give me a brown one instead, like the usual penny I offered to Maggie. With some hesitation, I picked up the brand new silver coin and, with considerable care, took it back home again, puzzled, but really quite happy, as long as I could come back with the brown one Maggie needed.

Sometimes, when Maggie was having her dinner, her brother Billy or his wife served in the shop. They were just as nice really, but Billy knew more about the nursery, where he worked with Mr York. His wife did her best and always got me what I wanted, but it was more of an occasion for me to be served by Maggie. After all, Maggie knew everything about what was in the shop and seemed to be able to attend to my every whim and still steer me on the right lines. Everybody was really fond of Maggie. She never married. Perhaps the man she had given her heart to had been killed in that War.

Fishing

It was a great pre-occupation of the lads of the village to go off on fishing expeditions in the spring. There was frogs' spawn to be collected, and later, tadpoles and small frogs. There were lots of small fish in the Ise River, minnows or even redbreasts. If you knew where to go in the Ironstone Pits, there were natural wells, full of newts. Down by the Mill, there were even trout.

One of the easiest places to find frogs' spawn was in a field just over the shaky bridge and in the Plens, where there was a pond where cows came to drink. The shaky bridge was a joy in itself. The Company had built a temporary wooden structure across their deep pit. This was made into a bridge by placing wide, wooden planks across as the pathway. This was given high open sides, which could be grasped as you crossed. Our main delight was, however, in bouncing up and down on the footway planks and making the whole structure shake. Our arrival at the pond could well be delayed by this major attraction. Even in the field before we got to the pond, there was a large horse-chestnut tree from which we could knock down conkers.

Those of us who were not diverted would carry a large jam jar held by string at the top and a paper cover to ensure the tadpoles did not escape, and find a shallow side of the pond, where we could collect the spawn. The aim was to take our catch to school the next day. One of the teachers, the only woman on the staff, who took 7–8 year-olds, was keen to teach us more about biology – how spawn changed into tadpoles, and tadpoles into little frogs. We could see the legs of the frogs grow daily in jam jars placed on the classroom shelf, helped by the sun and a little judicious feeding into their watery home.

There were other, more unusual creatures to be found in the wells, cut into the ironstone, perhaps where dynamite had been placed, when the workers wished to break away another layer of ironstone. One well was just below the shaky bridge, where mining had been finished and moved further out. There we could watch and wait for newts to come up for air. Beautiful colours under their bellies, but sometimes, they moved so quickly we just caught sight of their dark, lizard-like backs. When I did manage to catch them in the fish-net, I took them home in another enclosed jar and put them in the pond Grandad had made in the garden. Sometimes, they liked it and stayed. Others went off to find a better home.

At holiday times and even on Saturdays, we took sandwiches, walked down by the allotments below the Recreation Ground and crossed the fields to the bridge over the Ise. Near these, we knew there was a wonderful, quiet spot for catching small fish. We took with us home-made nets – bamboo sticks and wire to which the net was attached – to pull in our catch. The line was also home-made – an ash-stick, string and a bent pin to which we fixed a small worm or maggot. As soon as the fish had swallowed the bait, the stick bent and we gradually pulled the catch to the shore and netted it.

We learned where the fish were likely to be. Usually, in the shadow of the river-bank or in a particularly shady spot under trees. It was quite a thrill to watch the sun shimmering on the waves as the river flowed along. But it was no use trying to fish there. The fish avoided patches of sunlight and if one of them crossed there they would dart away so swiftly, you would never know where it had gone. There were patterns, too, in the shadow of the trees and sometimes we mistook a reflection for a fish. Either we could quietly marvel at the constant changes in the river as the sun moved across the sky or we could try to shut all that out and focus on the fish we had come to catch. Like most children, we were open to influences from all sides of life. We could marvel at the sudden display of nature above the water and still be fascinated by the antics of fish. At the end of the day, we were happy to go home, with quite a lot of fish in our jam jars. We would not have missed the pleasure of looking back over that familiar countryside at the River Ise getting smaller as we walked up the hill towards the church, watching the changing colours of the sunset as the sun grew redder and bigger until it touched the horizon.

Sadly, the fish did not survive long. We fed them daily, probably far too much. But clearly they did not care for life in a jam jar, probably too warm on a shelf in the sun. We found them every morning, stiff and floating on top. It may have been an enjoyable enterprise down by the river and coming home with our catch, but it was a sad, sad end to an exciting story.

A Very Short Horror Story

We had been warned by Grandfather not to go down Buckwell Street, just below the old, stone Town Cross. There was a small piece of ground, which the Council had bought and set up with swings, where children that end of the town could play. It was an easy alternative to the Recreation Ground, which was some distance away and involved a walk through town. Something quite unforeseen had happened at the new playground, but Grandfather preferred not to tell us what. Naturally, that made us even more curious. We made no promises, but decided we would have to investigate quite soon.

Strange, you may think, that, within days, we found ourselves pulled towards Buckwell Street. Maybe, we had been sent on an errand to the Post Office or had been looking down the High Street to see whether Reggie Meen, the famous boxer, was training at the Talbot Inn. Whatever had drawn us to that area, it was an opportunity to stroll down Buckwell Street.

Some years earlier, there had been a toll gate at the top of the hill. Buckwell Street was a cut-through on the main road between Harborough and Kettering. It was the best way to avoid going down the High Street and past the church. But, before the toll gate, it had been just a rough local street, full of ruts and places where carts or horse-drawn coaches could get stuck. When it became part of the main turnpike road, the Council had to raise enough money to make it fit to carry much more traffic, hence the toll gate. This gate and the keeper's cottage had now been removed. An old notice, demanding tolls from travellers, still remained on display in the keeper's old house.

We were reading this notice, when a friendly-looking man came out and asked if we were looking for somebody. We said 'No, but we heard there is a children's playground down here.'

'You'll not be from Desborough then?' he asked. We said we were, but that we lived on the Rushton Road side and hadn't been down Buckwell Street before.

'Right enough,' he told us, 'but you won't find much doing there, at the moment.'

'We just wanted to look,' was our rejoinder.

'Right then. Off you go, but watch out for the traffic. Keep to the left-hand side and just where the road bends, at the entrance to Humfrey's Farm, that's where the swings are. But, they've been tied up for a while. You won't be able to get on 'em.'

We thanked him and set off. Sure enough, at the entrance to the farm and on a piece of land higher up, were the swings, almost brand-new. I could imagine sitting on the wooden seat, with Arthur standing up behind me and holding on to the two metal chairs, fixed to an iron cross-bar above. There was plenty of space to get the swing really high in the air. Maybe we would see the church from there. We crossed the road and climbed up, only to find the seats and their supporting chains had been fixed to the side supports. It was impossible to get them free and enjoy ourselves for a bit. Something of a disappointment. Regretfully, we turned back towards the Cross, only to meet the man who had told us where the playground was. Why were the swings tied up like that?

'It's a sad story.' he replied. 'They were left loose to begin with, but, one night Humfreys' cows got out of the field above and came down to investigate. Some of them were young heifers and you know what they're like – always into trouble, curious to find out all about them swings. Whilst they were larking about, pushing each other into the swings, one little devil got itself tangled in them chains. Instead of quietly getting itself out, it went mad, twisting and turning. It busted the wooden seat, tried to shake off the chains, but only succeeded in making the chains tighter round its neck. You would have thought somebody would hear the racket it was causing and go to investigate, but it was night time and all decent people were tucked up in bed.'

He paused for a moment, possibly wondering whether he should tell us the outcome.

'Maybe you can guess what happened. Curiosity killed the cat. That young heifer went on thrashing about most of the night, they say. By morning, it had hung itself in the chains of the swing. Poor little devil!'

'Mr Humfreys wasn't too pleased, when he found his young beast dead as a door-nail. The Council will have to pay him compensation, and for the time being, at least, they have tied up the swings and asked children to stay away. A very sad story, don't you think?'

We had to agree. Grandad had warned us to stay away from Buckwell Street. He was right. We set off home, gloomy and reflective. A young animal's death, in such circumstances, seemed totally unnecessary.

The Corset Factory

The CWS Corset Factory was the pride of Desborough. It had been built on the outskirts of the town in the early 1900s and employed several hundreds of women, who fancied the idea of making fashionable corsets rather than boots and shoes. A few men had jobs in the office, in the cutting-room or doing some of the heavy work.

The style of the corsets was a feature of the time and would seem impossibly restrictive nowadays. They were called Desbeau Spiral Corsets and advertisements of the time read:

> Rare springiness and flexibility are given to Desbeau Corsets by the use of Spiral Steels, which are unbreakable, never rust and assure comfortable support to the figure without undue compression.

The CWS had decided to build this factory on the Rothwell Road because Desborough was already strongly cooperative and owned a freehold estate of 400 acres, on which the factory could be built. It was, compared with many of the boot and shoe factories, well built, light and bright. A two-storey building with windows looking out on to the road.

Whenever we went down there, we could see the women working away at their benches, but they always had enough time to stop and wave to us. For a time my aunt Doris worked there, before she became a piano teacher. We got to know her special friends, two Nellies, really well. Nellie Coker lived at the Keeper's Cottage in Bram Wood and came down to see us on her bike. Nellie Ginns was also particularly nice to us and used to invite us to visit her family down by the Recreation Ground. All the back gardens down there were well kept and interesting – rows of vegetables and fruit for the asking.

If it was a break-time when we were passing the factory, the women would come out and talk to us. They would tell us to take a walk up the hill in Federation Avenue to Spion Cop and all the allotments there. The names of the streets had been handed down from the Boer War. Parallel to Federation Avenue was Pioneer Avenue. That, later on, was a street I visited regularly, where my teacher A. J. lived.

Grandad had another allotment at the top of that road, some distance from the factory. It was mostly given over to fruit trees. That meant we didn't need to climb the hill every week to find out whether the apples and pears were ready to pick. When the time came, Grandad would get out his heavy, home-made truck, with creaking metal wheels, oil the wheels to make them turn more easily and fix a kind of shoulder harness, with which he held the back of the truck off the ground. He contended it was easier than carrying the full weight on his arms. I could only just manage to lift it, without any load inside. It seemed unbelievable that Grandad could lift it, fully loaded, push it uphill back to Regent Street over a mile away and also hold it back securely enough to stop it running away downhill.

It was easy enough taking the truck from the allotment down to the Corset Factory but once round the corner, it was really heavy going uphill to the Cenotaph – always a good place to pause for breath. Then past the old Congregational Chapel, in sharp contrast to the more modern narrow 3-storey factory in Paddock Lane. The church sat solidly on its sandstone foundation but the boot and shoe factory, brick-built, looked ready to fall down any time.

Another, not so steep, climb, then travelling past the iron railings of the Girls' School, past the gasometers, another butcher's shop and the site designated for a new Congregational Chapel.

Worst of all, it seemed, was the final stretch up Regent Street, past the boot and shoe factory, with the men cheering wildly, past Maggie York's shop and then home, at last. It was as much as we could manage to push the truck up the side path, squeeze it through the gate and leave it outside the back door.

Invariably, Grandma and Mother would reprove Grandad for trying to bring home so much in that impossible truck. Grandad was looking very red sweating profusely. There was good reason to be concerned. Grandad, not to be bossed around, left the truck where it was, went inside and sat in his armchair, switching on the wireless for the news. He certainly looked flushed but smiled, knowingly, at me.

'We managed it, all right, didn't we? Where's the tea, then?' he asked.

There was nothing for it, Grandma realized, but to put the kettle on.

The Premier Tailor

I was turning out a glory hole, the other day, when an old wooden clothes hanger fell down and, as they say, gave me a clip over the ear-hole. Not to my liking, but it was, I saw, a beautifully preserved, carefully cut piece of wood, with its metal hook driven through the centre. It was intended to be used for hanging a jacket on. Printed on the side of the wood, still as clear as when the imprint was made, were the words 'Doffman Premier Tailor (Kettering).' It must have belonged to my grandfather, always proud to wear his Sunday-best suit when he played the Church organ.

My brother and I went with Mother to our own village tailor, usually once a year, for our best suits. We would stare for a long time through the shop window until the tailor himself came out, plump and elderly, wearing his tape measure over his shoulder, and invited us to come inside. He might offer some new light-grey material, this year's fashion but rather expensive, or some of his material in stock, maybe a check pattern, but not too loud, to suit Mother's choice. Mother might go home to think about it, but if she thought it was the right time to buy, we would be allowed to say which we liked best. Having selected the material, we were carefully measured, across the shoulders, round the waist, leg length and arm length. We had to settle the lapel shape and even the number of buttons and button-holes. It was a remarkably careful and thorough business, ending at last with choice of linings. In those days, when few underpants were worn, linings had to be selected for short and long trousers, as well as for the jacket. That was, by no means, the end of the tailoring. I had to go back to try on the unfinished suit. It was hard to believe that this weird-looking jacket, with its sub-structure still exposed, would eventually make a smart suit. It was happily always ready just in time for the Sunday School Anniversary.

On that day, usually in mid-summer, girls and boys, not to mention adults, appeared in their family pews, expecting to make an impression, not only with their singing, but also with their new plumage. Girls facing towards the congregation from treble and alto choir pews were evidently there to be admired by would-be suitors. It worked, too. Many a young man plucked up courage, after the service, to propose a walk down a local, leafy lane known as The Folly. It was, often, the beginning of courtship and marriage.

There were other side-lines which went with a new suit. It was a time to have family photographs taken. My brother and I were taken to a rather classy photographer in Kettering to sit for some special occasion, perhaps a birthday. It was a formal affair. The shop window was full of children who had been photographed there. My brother stood by my side, whilst I sat in a chair. In our first such photograph, my brother was wearing his new suit, whilst I, then only 3 years-old, sat dressed in a frock, then much favoured for young children who were still not yet going to school. Babyhood was still kept as long as possible, if the child was fortunate enough, as I was, to be blest with a head of curly hair.

A new suit or dress also provided the occasion to visit another high-class shop. Palmers supplied the piano my aunt had in our front room. They also had an interesting assortment of wind and string instruments and brass. It was also the place where I went for my early music exams, with the Trinity College of Music examiner there from London for the occasion. I could also buy strings for my violin. But, for my higher exams, after I had collected all the certificates I could from Kettering, I had to go to Leicester.

It was a big station, such as I had not seen before, with my aunt as accompanist. We had to find Russells the Music Shop, quite near the station and then go right to a back room, where the examiner could listen in peace and quiet. He came from the College of Violinists and didn't miss much in the music I played. Did my aunt and I play together a great deal, he asked, when we had played a Mozart sonata. I said we had and he then pointed out that we were doubling the speed of two bars of long notes and semi-breves were getting near to minims in length. We always took care to count such bars in the future. I must have been in too much of a hurry to get to the main theme again.

As we walked back to the station, I noticed that the high-class tailors in London Road had even more lavishly-adorned clothes hangers.

Intermission

This series of stories about my childhood began with a foreword addressed to my great-granddaughter, Jodie. Looking at her now, I begin to wonder if musical talent is inborn. Certainly, a child is never too young to respond to good music. Even the un-born child, growing in mother's womb, responds to Mozart. Some contend it develops high intelligence, which can be put to use in any walk of life. As I watch Jodie sit up and try to discover where pleasing sounds come from, responding to their rhythm and the games I play with her, it seems she has certainly inherited the same response and delight in musical sounds. When I clap my hands together in a regular rhythm, sometimes loud, sometimes soft, she already tries her hardest to copy me. When I respond to her squeals of delight, with a whistle at the same pitch, she immediately joins in this new game.

Is her pleasure in taking part with me in some of these basics of music, a sign that, for her too, it will become a life-long passion? Will she become a violinist like me or does that already strong voice point to a future preference for singing? In any event, I am sure her parents will be keen to help her in the direction she wishes to go. It is not easy for any child to know for sure what that is. Some may decide to combine music with a different, but worthwhile, career. Many doctors, after their long training, still find deep enjoyment in playing the violin regularly. Singers, who are also mothers, must somehow combine their two passions.

The future is always unknown and unravels slowly. The elderly may cherish their own thoughts, the young will survive long enough to see them realized.

Minuet in G

BEETHOVEN

Music – A Lifetime's Obsession

I was fortunate to be born into a musical family. Grandfather was a cellist and church organist. Elsie and Doris, two of his daughters, were pianists and later church organists. The third daughter, my mother Evelyn, would have liked to play the piano, but, with a young family and a large share of housework, helping Grandma at 4 Regent Street, she didn't really have an opportunity to learn. The three of them, like Grandma and Grandad, were small in size. We could just manage to see Elsie and Doris above us, when they were playing the Chapel organ.

The only son, Arthur, was a good violinist, but he had been killed, about the same time as my father, in the First World War. Grandad had bought his violin, a beautiful French instrument, from Rushworth and Dreaper, a music business in Liverpool. The violin was now Arthur's memorial and carefully preserved in an upstairs cupboard in Grandad and Grandma's bedroom. It was, from an early age, my ambition to play that treasured Jacquot.

I soon formed the habit, with Grandad, of listening to music on the wireless. Violinists were my favourite. Albert Sammons, regarded then as Britain's outstanding performer, gave recitals regularly. Grandad also enjoyed the Sunday evening concerts from Palm Court, Eastbourne. Albert Sandler was the violinist leading a string band. On Saturday nights, we could also enjoy Jack Payne and the BBC Dance Band. I was beginning to get a taste for a whole range of string players.

At 6, I had to learn the piano. Doris was teaching most nights several young people, in the front room. It was not surprising that I was expected to try the piano too. At least, I would learn to read the notes on the stave.

Somehow, the piano never appealed to me. I found it too mechanical, its keys fixed in tones and semi-tones. I simply had to press the right ones. There was no scope for changing the warmth of a note, once it had been pressed. Little scope, it seemed to me, for expressing my personality, as violinists and singers did. By the time I was 7 I had had enough. I was waiting for the chance to play Uncle Arthur's violin.

I did not have to wait much longer. The great day arrived when A. J., my schoolteacher, a gold-medallist and Fellow of the College of Violinists, announced he was starting a class after school for boys to learn the violin. An outfit would be provided, including a violin and bow of a suitable size, accord-

Playing my violin in the orchard.

ing to how big each boy was. This would cost 1/6d a week, plus 1/- a lesson. We were told to consult our parents and preferably bring a note back of their agreement. Sadly, I would have to make do with a half-size violin, with every prospect, as I grew bigger, of eventually being given the Jacquot.

A. J. was deputy-head of the Boys' School and well-liked. He was in touch with all the best violinists in the country including my hero, Albert Sammons, who had founded the College of Violinists, so that promising young players could be taught and examined by the country's best violinists. He was a relative of Grandma and well-known in the area for his outstanding concert performances, especially to raise funds for churches and chapels and good causes of various kinds. For me, the new venture was an unbelievable opportunity.

I ran all the way home during the dinner hour to break the news. On the Rushton Road, I caught up with Grandad and some of his mates going back home for dinner, from the factory in Harborough Road. After hovering impatiently behind for a while, I broke into the group of adults, joking and chatting cheerfully together, intent, all the same, to get home as soon as possible. Dinner could not wait. They had to be home on time and back to work.

'Grandad! Grandad!' I called out as loudly as I dare, 'A violin class is being started at school. Could I join?'

Grandad took me by the shoulder, stopped talking to his mates and drew me closer to him.

'A violin class?' asked Grandad, incredulous, 'Who is the teacher then?'

'A. J.!' I replied briefly, 'There's nobody else.'

'Hmm. Sounds pretty good. We'll have to ask your Mam about it.'

Grandad was clearly pleased and had made up his mind already.

It didn't take long to persuade Mam over dinner. I could scarcely eat mine and soon broke off and ran back to school. It seemed hours before the bell rang and we lined up in the playground to go back into our classes. I could tell A. J. that yes, I wanted to join and Mam agreed. A few days later, I came home proudly carrying my half-size violin. I couldn't play it yet, but I seemed to be opening and closing its case continuously, to show relations curious to know what was going to happen at the school.

My first lesson was unforgettable. Boys, of all ages and sizes, assembled in the main classroom, waiting to start. A. J. came in, smiling and welcoming everybody, took out his violin, tuned it and, after a brief introduction, showed us how to hold the violin and bow, and how to produce a pleasing sound, simply by drawing the bow across open strings.

Brother Arthur (cellist) and I outside the back door of 4 Regent Street.

Young Men's Congregational band outside the Church.

'To begin with,' explained A. J., 'we'll only use our left hand to hold the violin. Now take your bow like this and we'll see what kind of noise we make, simply by drawing the bow over an open string.' A. J. made everything clear and made sure every one of us was doing what he wanted. I think we spent the whole of that first lesson playing each string in turn, G, D, A, E, four times on each, until we began to produce a reasonable sound.

We tackled more difficult things week by week. How to hold the neck of the violin, so as to leave all four fingers of the left hand bent naturally over the strings. How to adjust each finger to play in time and change the spacing between fingers, according to the key we were trying to achieve. How to leave the hand free enough to move higher up the neck of the fiddle, when we began learning to play higher notes.

Some of us, naturally, succeeded better than others in learning how to cope with unfamiliar tasks. The keen ones took to practising at home and were impatient to have to wait a week to show A. J. how they were improving. Very soon, a few of us were picked out and offered private lessons. An hour a week, with A. J.'s undivided attention, for 2/- a week! Progress was rapid. My enthusiasm grew week by week. I learned how to place my fingers accurately on each string and move them around for various scales and exercises. My tone improved simultaneously. I was given my first tutor – Farmer's *How to play the violin* with popular pieces mixed in with exercises on technique.

At last, A. J. considered we could try performing in public. First, performance with parents and friends, then our first appearance in public – maybe the Church Hall.

A big step forward for me, was an invitation from a local organist, Fred Barlow, to play with him at Rothwell Methodist Church. The church seemed exceptionally big the first time I arrived there, to play with Fred. He sat up aloft on the organ, whilst I stood alone down on the platform adjoining the pews. The acoustic was unfamiliar, too, but the church became warmer and more friendly as it filled up. The occasion was daunting enough, I cannot now remember what I played. But the organist never let me down and seemed to help me over difficult passages. It was, of course, a great thrill to listen to the applause which followed. Fred thanked me and said I must come again. In the meantime, he promised he would be sending a small present in the post.

He, in fact, sent me what I considered a really generous present, a whole group of pieces for violin and keyboard, to add to my repertoire. One of them became quite a favourite in the Desborough and Rothwell area – Massenet's 'Meditation'. 'Ave Maria' came later, as an extra present from Fred. At 10, my

Doris, my youngest aunt and my accompanist on the piano.

teacher A. J. entered me for the local Eisteddfod in a class 'up to 14 year-olds.' In an even bigger hall than the church, the Baths Hall, I had to stand in front of a big audience and play Beethoven's Minuet in G, accompanied by Aunt Doris on the piano. Several more entrants, all older than me, followed, the adjudicator making notes about each performance and signalling the next performer to begin. All the entrants, meantime, stood anxiously waiting at the side of the platform.

After all of us had played the Minuet as well as we could, the adjudicator completed his notes, shuffled his papers together and walked leisurely to the front of the platform. He began his summing up, being careful to give praise where it was due and to offer suggestions for next year's performance. Finally, he came to me. At first, I thought it must be because my name came towards the end of the alphabet. But then, I realized with amazement, he was heaping praise on this youngest of the performers. The final announcement came, with much applause, I had won the First Prize. It was quite an effort for Aunt Doris and me to gather the music, my violin and everything else together and leave for home.

Some weeks later, an interesting package arrived addressed to Master Trevor Woolston. Obviously, something unusual. It was a Silver Medal, with my name inscribed on the back, along with the date and details of the event. If only I had a gold watch-chain, like Grandad, with an opal jewel hanging from it, I could hang my silver medal on it. Well, I would make do with a silver chain until I was really grown-up.

Leaving aside that competitive area for the time being, I had joined the Young Men's Bible Class which met in the church every Sunday afternoon. Not the boring affair you might think. We were fortunate enough to have some imaginative and go-ahead leaders. One of these was Bernard Kemp, a stout choir-master keen to get us all singing in harmony. He was also a good double bass player and had already taught his son, Frank, to take his place in the orchestra when he was conducting.

The idea grew that there were enough good players in the class to form an orchestra. They would meet regularly and give concerts, in aid of church funds, in the Sunday School. I was asked to lead the band, with my friend, Norman Bosworth and several others forming the fiddle section. My Sunday School teacher took up the viola, brother Arthur the cello and my cousin Howard on the piano, Frank Kemp on double bass and Mervyn Elkington on clarinet made up a cohesive group.

After practising for weeks, our conductor pronounced us competent enough to perform *the Gondoliers* by Sullivan in public. We had to think of other things to make up the expected two hours of entertainment. Howard offered piano solo and with him, I would play violin and piano duets. Norman then had the brilliant idea of introducing some comic relief. I was set up in front of the curtain to give a long recital of a rather dreary poem, only to be interrupted by Norman's constant 'Hello, hello, hello! Did you know?' It was a highly popular device in London Music Halls at that time. To give what they thought would add a little solidity to the evening, the daughters of one of our factory owners and Sunday School teachers themselves, offered sketches for us to learn and perform. It was, at least, an opportunity for some of us to show our acting skills.

Some of these sketches included women heroines. Since our group was formed for a Young Men's Bible Class, we were sadly lacking young women actresses. Norman at once proposed that he and I, when required, should dress as young women and see what we could make of the parts. Anything for a laugh, I agreed and surprised myself and the audience with a new side to my acting ability. I might well have been intended to pose as, for example, a demure and high-class lady. It made no difference, even though I attempted to adopt a false voice. The audience had no difficulty in recognizing me below a wealth of clothing. It didn't matter if the part was intended to be serious. The sketch ended in roars of laughter.

About that time, too, I had read several posters in the window of a tin-hut in the Recreation Ground. The hut belonged to the Council and had been used for a variety of fringe activities, including its conversion into a small isolation hospital for the only local victim of small-pox. That was the usual method of dealing with small-pox in those days. However, once again it was being used for normal purpose – for the local St John Ambulance group, for voluntary organizations, any of which were allowed to display posters inside. The one poster that stood out for me was an offer of scholarships to promising local musicians to study at London colleges. It was probably the Trinity College of Music as the main attraction. My Aunt Doris was an Associate of this college, which also ran the area grade examinations. Was this highly unusual offer an opportunity for me? Sadly, no. Neither A. J. nor my mother were in favour. A. J. reasonably enough, was reluctant to lose one of his star pupils (a good advert for a really good teacher) and mother was not at all keen for me to leave her and go to London. There were practical difficulties, in any case. She could hardly afford to pay for me to live there, with only a war widow's small pension for all of us to live on.

I was forced to abandon that dream and concentrate on winning a scholarship to the local Grammar School. Arthur was already there, with Howard, both on a fee-paying basis. It seemed as though I was destined for the academic rather than the musical world. As it happened I did win a scholarship and found at Kettering I could join the school orchestra and soon became its leader. It was, evidently, possible to have the best of both worlds.

A. J., A Teacher to Remember

A. J., deputy head of the Desborough Boys' School, had been a source of inspiration to me since I was 7 and had joined his newly-formed class for budding violinists. I then had private lessons with him. By the time I was 9 and had been 'put up' rather swiftly to his class, where the pupils were older, I had got to know him quite well.

He was a man to be respected for his attention to detail, a necessary virtue in all good musicians. Helpful, at all times. When I had to learn new pieces, I began with playing them from sight. Then I would be asked what mood the composer was aiming at, and whether that mood changed from time to time. Technical detail then followed to establish how best to achieve the composer's aims. If the piece was being prepared for performance, for a competition like the Eisteddfod, for example, A. J. would, eventually, demonstrate how he thought I would achieve what the adjudicator expected. His view might be that the bowing should be in a certain style, staccato on the string or spiccato, off the string, but certainly not legato or sentimental. No excessive vibrato or slides, that would be entirely wrong for the baroque composer. At times, but rarely, A. J.'s interpretation did not produce the result I was seeking. Generally speaking, the adjudicator agreed with A. J. Bowing determined the nature of a piece of music. I had to become versatile enough to produce the best sound to convince an audience.

A. J. certainly steered me on the right lines, as evidence from the local paper, the Kettering Leader seems to show. It is headed:

A CLEVER BOY VIOLINIST

> Harold Trevor Woolston of Regent Street, Desborough, who earlier in the year passed with honours the Higher Local Examination of the Trinity College of Music and was awarded the Centre Prize for violin playing, has just been notified that he has passed, again with honours, the examination for the Diploma of the Associate of the College of Violinists, attaining 92 marks out of a possible 100, a few weeks after attaining the earliest possible age of 15 years. This most promising young violinist is a pupil of Mr A. J. Hawes.

By the time this appeared in the weekly paper, I was at the Kettering

Grammar School leading the School Orchestra. But some 6 years earlier, my range of interests were being extended in other ways. A. J. was not only a brilliant performer on the violin, he could keep a whole class breathless with his acting ability. First, in playing 'many parts' of Shakespeare. *The Merchant of Venice* provided ample scope.

A. J. would stand transformed into Shylock in front of the class.

'Hath not a Jew eyes? Hath not a Jew hands, organs, dimensions, senses, affections, passions? ... If you prick us, do we not bleed? If you tickle us, do we not laugh? If you poison us, do we not die?'

None of us, by this age, had had any real experience of Jews, nor of anti-Semitism. But with such a man, alive in front of us, we felt we would instantly recognize Shylock, should we meet him in later life.

A. J. had the same facility for playing women's parts. When Portia, a doctor of law, appeared on the scene, it seemed at first she was agreeing with Shylock's demand for 'his bond.' For this, she was commended by Shylock.

We who watched had no experience of court procedure. That kind of thing was miles away, maybe at Northampton. But we were quick to learn from A. J.'s vivid portrayal of Portia:

'The quality of mercy is not strain'd,
It droppeth as the gentle rain from heaven
Upon the place beneath: it is twice blest;
It blesseth him that gives and him that takes'

We followed every change of mood and gesture until the transformation of Portia into the strict judge.

'Tarry a little; there is something else.
This bond doth give thee here no jot of blood'

What would happen next? Probably, A. J. paused there and asked if anyone would like to come out in front and read one of these passages to the rest of the class. Some venturesome lad, maybe me, would go out and try to imitate what A. J. had shown of the characters. When volunteers failed to come out in front, A. J. would close the book, but promise more another day. That intensive experience soon converted every one of us into keen Shakespeareans.

For a change, A. J. would switch to Dickens. Charles Dickens was then a great favourite in all middle-class homes. Dickens had worked on the *Daily News*, later to become the *News Chronicle*, when two papers merged. To keep and maybe to extend its number of readers, the Editor offered a new edition of Dickens'

Complete Works at a very cheap price. Bookshelves were filled with some 15 volumes, all guaranteed to impress the neighbours and maybe attract more orders.

A. J.'s favourite was *The Christmas Carol* and part of our class's Christmas celebrations, we all listened, with bated breath, as A. J. charted the character of Scrooge, from miser to a reformed and generous friend of poor families. It seemed most unlikely that a dyed-in-the-wool growler would ever change his penny-pinching ways or his treatment of this one remaining employee, Bob Cratchit. A. J., out in front of us, steered the way through the spine-chilling visits of the ghosts of Jacob Marley, his former partner, of Christmas Past, Christmas Present and Christmas Yet to Come. From Scrooge's instant dismissal of Christmas and all forms of generosity with his automatic 'Bah Humbug!' to his eye-opener in visiting the Cratchit family at home, with the Ghost of Christmas Present.

'A Merry Christmas to us all, my dears! God bless us,' says Bob Cratchit. To which poor, crippled Tiny Tim adds 'God bless us, every one!'

The change is taking place before our eyes, but is hastened by the appearance of the Ghost of Christmas Yet to Come and the visit to the graveyard. Business men discuss a recent death and A. J. changes character accordingly.

'What's he done with his money?' comes from a red-faced gentleman.

'He hasn't left it to me. That's all I know,' replies another.

A. J.'s versatility, in the swift changes needed to act these varied characters, astounded us all. Occasionally, we would take a fancy to one or other of these Dickens characters and attempt to act them out, in front of our classmates. But that presented a great temptation to those watching to make fun of us.

A. J. was always convincing. He might almost have inherited the talents of Italian Commedia del Arte. His fiddling reminded us, at times, of Mediterranean temperament. It could easily have spilled over into his acting. His message came over clearly. There was a great deal more to learn from life as we grew up.

Uncle Harry

A rather special relative of mine was Uncle Harry, Harry Page, Grandma's brother. He was, as they say, a lovely man, as you would expect Grandma's brother to be. The best, the very best cobbler in town. In fact, he was so popular, it was often difficult to squeeze in through the shop door. The shop was just below the Co-op butchers in King Street and next door to the house where Harry and Grandma lived as children. Things there were now very different. Grandad Page had married again, after his first wife's death, and now had another grown-up family. Two older boys, Will and Fred, had married and lived down south, near London. Will and his wife lived on a farm, but had no children. I had several holidays later with them, and they would have liked to adopt me. Fortunately, Mother would have none of that! There was one unmarried daughter, Margaret, now living next door to Uncle Harry and she, occasionally, came to visit us. Margaret had been a children's nurse for an aristocratic family and was well versed in how both children and adults should behave. There was something in Margaret's style and behaviour, which Grandma had too. It was noticeable at family meal-times. Everybody was expected to be polite, to wait their turn, learn how the table should be set and how to use cutlery properly.

Uncle Harry was different. Small and wiry, always full of fun and obviously enjoying his work and the company. He sat behind his solid wooden bench on a high stool and handled the shoe being repaired like an old friend, deftly moving it to and fro, to judge what was needed. Soling a shoe was quite easy for him. First, tear off the old sole with pliers and drop it into the bin. Then, check that the insole and the rest of the shoe are strong enough to have a shining new sole hammered into them. That was a quick preliminary. Then the tricky part. Uncle Harry added a few more tacks to those already hidden in the corner of his mouth, brought them to the front of his mouth and placed the shining new sole squarely on the shoe, now fixed to his metal last. A few tacks just to hold it in place on the upper. Then swiftly each tack extracted from his mouth and hammered in right around the sole. There would be some overhang of the new on the old. Uncle Harry quickly took the shoe off the last and with a vicious-looking knife rapidly cut all the way round to produce a smooth edge. A kind of treadmill underneath the bench operated by the foot would be used to smooth the rough edges. To finish off and make it as good as new, the new sole had to be stained black to look like a new shoe. A quick final check by Uncle Harry's keen eyes and then the name was chalked on the side and put on the side for the owner to collect and pay.

That was a wonderful bench, Uncle Harry's. It had everything a cobbler needed. Lots of drawers on both sides of the central gap. All the different tools carefully laid there ready to be brought out when a particular job demanded one or other.

I was there for a purpose and felt the importance of the occasion. I had to collect or take shoes for repair for all the family. If I didn't get it right, somebody else would have to call specially and I didn't want that disgrace. I learned by watching everything that went on and after a time, I really felt I knew everything anybody needed to know about shoe repairs. How to cut out the various parts, to stitch them together and make a new upper. There was, for experts like Uncle Harry, a shining Singer sewing machine, one of the latest models, standing in the corner of the shop. Uncle Harry used this machine to repair uppers, which had worn through and broken the stitches. It was to be expected that the thread would give way when asked to cope with excessive wear and tear. But the finishing off and final appearance of a shoe was just as important to a customer as the rest of the work carried out to begin with.

Whilst all this was going on, I listened fascinated by the group of old men gathered in a semi-circle round the side of Uncle Harry's bench. They had, no doubt, now retired from the boot and shoe factories, but having lived and worked there all their life, they felt entitled to pronounce on current goings-on in their town. One would begin with some scandal he had heard about Ronnie Ginns' girl and what she had been up to at the weekend with a Rowell chap. Another would cap that story with his inside knowledge about the church secretary at the Baptist Church across the road opposite. He could confirm that this pillar of the church had lost lots of money through dealing in shares on the Stock Exchange. Who in the whole of Desborough would dream of dabbling with such dubious practices, let alone this professed Christian?

Much of this went over my head, but it sounded very impressive, as one piece of scandal followed another. But I had listened long enough and waited to ask Uncle Harry if he had finished repairing Grandad's shoes. Finally, he would break off from his cronies, hand the shoes back and say Grandad could call in and pay for them sometime when he was passing.

There was a pattern and a trust about these things, which was readily passed on in this tight-knit community. I felt I was learning a lot, just by spending an hour in Uncle Harry's shop, listening, watching and even occasionally joining in.

A Day Out with the Family

We were always a closely knit family, with links throughout Desborough, on my mother's side. It was natural that the relatives we knew best were where our home was. Relatives on my father's side, I would get to know better when travelling to Rowell, 2 miles away, was less of a problem.

I got to know the Desborough relatives and to pick out those I liked best, when we all got together for the Christmas celebrations. There were other people I had met, who often turned out to be distantly related. Clearly we couldn't invite all those people, as well as those we met every day. Aunt Elsie, Uncle Fred and Howard lived in the next street. Elsie called on her parents every day, without fail. Uncle Fred exchanged a word or two as he came through to go to the factory. Howard was one of our playmates. It was the same with Uncle Harry, Grandma's brother, whom we called on regularly at his cobbler's shop in the High Street. His wife, Lois, and Miriam his daughter, we would often meet in Havelock Street on the way to and from school. Aunt Julia, his unmarried sister, always came round after tea, sat herself firmly in the seat just inside the living room door and talked endlessly. These two families were enough to fill our house at Christmas. Indeed, there was hardly room to move. The children had to find themselves a space in one of the downstairs rooms and stay there until we were told we could come and eat.

High tea, it was called. Ham and tongue, pork pies and sausage rolls. Mustard, chutney and pickled onion for those who were partial to such extras. Plenty of bread and butter too. This was carefully cut into buttered slices and then cut again into triangles and offered, almost as a separate course. It was, no doubt, one way of satisfying large appetites. But when tinned fruit appeared – usually half cuts of peaches – we were expected to accompany it with more bread and butter.

To finish, we would be offered Grandma's special tarts and mince pies. If it was your very first mince pie that Christmas, you had to stay silent until it was all eaten. You could then have a wish, which had to be a secret nobody else could be told.

After tea, we all packed into the two main rooms downstairs and started to organize games. As soon as these got going, all was quiet to begin with. Very soon lot of laughter and fun followed. We would begin with quiet guessing games – 'I Spy, something beginning with ...' 'What is this, I've got hidden in my hand?' 'I'll give you one minute to see these little objects I have. How many can you remember when I cover them up?' With people divided into two rooms, we could keep one group happy playing Consequences. Two names would be written on a piece of paper given to each person taking part. The paper was then folded over and passed on. A build-up to the two persons first named getting married and the consequence was ... Another group, limited by the number of packs of cards available, might be absorbed in playing Happy Families, in which players got together as many families as possible, e.g. Mr and Mrs Baker, Master Baker and Miss Baker, or the Plumber, the Doctor and the Banker. The winner had the most families, acquired by swapping cards with neighbours.

Later on, somebody would be blind-fold, turned around several times and told to sit on somebody's knee. They then had to guess who it was. Finally, Charades would be proposed. A number of teams formed to take turns in presenting a secret word, a syllable at a time. That was sure to take up the rest of the evening, until one of our visitors announced it was time to go home. All the children immediately protested, but, after a few minutes' grace, were told to find their coats and get ready to go home.

Similar parties were held during Christmas week at Aunt Elsie's and Uncle Harry's homes, each keen to make their party different. Elsie, pianist and church organist, would organize a Sing-Song round her piano in the front room, whilst Miriam, fun-leader at Uncle Harry's, would get all the children to dress up in funny hats from crackers and wear false noses. Then all kinds of noisy games could be organized. Her favourite was to blind-fold two people, tell them to lie on the floor holding each other's left hand and then place a heavy roll of paper in the right hand of one of them. This one then asked the other 'Are you there, Moriarty?' whilst the other croaked a throaty reply and quickly rolled out of the place where he had been. The aggressor then tried to hit him over the head. If he failed and hit the floor, the other player took over the paper roll and tried his luck.

These parties were really exciting for us children and, as far as we were concerned, the main attraction of Christmas. But, at different times of the year, usually in springtime, our family organized special celebrations out in the country, in the sunshine and fresh air – long country walks. To me, as a child, these ventures were especially pleasurable. Every such whole-day trip took me into new worlds, almost like fairylands and with the feeling of security that having grown-ups with us gave.

It was, by no means, all fairyland. The Ironstone Company was tearing up acres of hitherto unspoilt land. Its huge diggers lowering immense scoops to scrape grassland off the layer of ironstone some way down. The desecration was magnified by useless sub-soil being dumped in hillocks behind. Acres of land were being ruined. There were lesser areas of woodland being cleared, too, allegedly because the wood needed to be sold to make it worthwhile for the landowner to set more young trees there. When even small pieces of woodland were cut down at the side of Pipewell Road, they could be left with brambles and rough bushes taking over. No sign of young trees replacing the old ones.

Some of the walks would take us only a short distance away from home. Perhaps something cropped up unexpectedly to delay progress. This could often happen, when we took the footpath across the Plens towards the Back Lane, where ironstone digging had stopped. There was, first of all, the shaky wooden bridge, suspended over the old ironstone cutting, which had been the first major work some years before. The children could never cross without setting the bridge shaking simply by bouncing up and down on the planks that supported anyone crossing to the coppice on the opposite side. Gazing over the side of the bridge, we could see unusual birds at work on the ironstone still left below. Sandpipers and martens making holes for their nests, with lots of small birds – chaffinches, greenfinches and yellowhammers – hard at work on nests in the coppice. In the meadows beyond, skylarks soared above, nests hidden in the long grass of the meadow, and the female sitting undisturbed on its small, but delicately patterned eggs. Sometimes, we were allowed to go into the coppice and find nests of all sorts. The small birds seemed to make the most interesting and carefully constructed nests, whereas pigeons and magpies used anything they could find. Cuckoos didn't even bother to do that. They simply took over other birds' nests, laid their eggs and left the mother bird to rear the young cuckoo, soon to take all the space in the nest.

We learned to distinguish blackbirds' eggs from thrushes' and chaffinches' from blue-tits' and robins'. The adults told us to leave the eggs in the nests, where we found them. Otherwise, the mother bird might forsake the nest and leave the young to die.

In the meadows, the adults were keen to look carefully for dark green grass that formed rings and stood out from the rest of the field. This was where they might find mushrooms. If they were ready to pick, they would knot the corners of their large, white handkerchiefs and make a soft bag in which the mushrooms could be carried without being damaged. Toadstools and horse mushrooms were considered uneatable and left to rot.

If we searched the field carefully, we could find some unusual orchids. Their flowers seemed unbelievable, with part of the delicate main stalk looking like a bird or a bee. After that voyage of discovery, we reached the Back Lane, climbed an old, but unusually robust stile, jumped the ditch on the other side and landed on the road. If we turned right for a short distance, although we really meant to turn left, we would find a very old oak, its trunk hollowed out by creatures that took refuge there. It had certainly been smoothed by generations of woodpeckers, by foxes and other animals seeking shelter. It was hundreds of years old and later on, we could imagine Charles I hiding there to escape Cromwell's soldiers. It was quite an achievement for me to scramble up the slippery inside surface and emerge in daylight again and poke my head up enough to be able to shout to my companions.

Turning back again, we looked over a very big and tempting mushroom field. There was a farm halfway across we later used to visit, when the children got to know us at school. The fear was, however, that the Ironstone Company wanted to dig that up too. Everybody in Desborough, except perhaps a few men who earned a living working for the Company, was against this. A great many letters on this subject appeared in the local paper.

Our next port of call was as the gamekeeper's cottage on the edge of Bram Wood. The gamekeeper, Mr Coker, and his family lived there. Mr Coker was always neat and tidy, wearing a small moustache, which seemed to proclaim his connections with local gentry who owned the woods. He was responsible for a wide area of woodland and surrounding fields. The ridings, where huntsmen wanted to ride down, had to be kept tidy and clear of brambles. But he had to ensure that foxes in the woods did not kill his own hens. The gentry wanted them kept alive for fox-hunting days. Mr Coker knew the habits of foxes very well and showed us a pool on the edge of the woods, where they and other animals came to drink early every morning.

His wife and two daughters met us, expecting us to stay for tea. It always seemed to be a sunny day there on the edge of the wood. We had tea and cakes out of doors. Nellie and Connie had worked with Doris in the Corset Factory, and were always pleased to see us any time we cared to turn up. The one son, Jack, like me, the youngest of the family, was a mechanic at a garage in Market Harborough. A man of gentle temperament, with all the patience in the world, when driving a car. Many years later, I had the benefit of being taught to drive by Jack and we soon became firm friends. It was Jack who found the right car for me when I first learned to drive. It was a spotless Ford 8 (the one with the well-known bucket radiator), second-hand, but as good as new and remarkably cheap.

Maybe it was when Mr Coker retired that they had to leave the lodge where they had been tenants and come to live in Rushton Road, very near to us. Everybody was pleased about this, even though we could no longer visit them at Bram Wood. Nellie and Connie had bikes to go to work on and Jack drove a bit further to his garage at Market Harborough. Sometimes he took us with him on his half-day and showed us the race course just past Bram Wood, below the Harborough Road, where hunters used to race on bank holidays. They called it Dingley Dell. We frequently watched the racing from the field above. At other times, we followed the hunt as it came tearing across fields, jumping hedges and gates, in a wild attempt to catch a fox.

There was another memorable occasion, when a whole day's outing had been planned. The aim was to cover a circuitous route beginning north of Pipewell and turning west along the Welland valley. Then south again, back towards

Bram Wood and finally across the fields and home. As usual, Aunt Elsie, Uncle Fred and Howard would be with us, and Uncle Harry, Lois and Miriam and Aunt Julia had no intention of being left out. We took masses of food and drink with us, but expected to rely for water on springs or village taps, which every small village had thoughtfully made accessible to travellers. Having distributed the load between the strongest members of the party, we set off up the Pipewell Road. There were to be no stops until we had covered 2 miles beyond that village. There were plenty of temptations to stop and look at things of interest on this first stage. Farms and families we knew, Pipewell Hall and little churches, and of course Pipewell Wood, with its masses of flowers and hidden animals. But somehow, we managed to keep going. Grouping changed from time to time, as people tired and dropped behind. Grandma and Grandad, joined by Uncle Harry, led to begin with but later gave way to younger ones. The children tried hard to get in front, especially on the hills. Eventually, honour was satisfied and a halt was called on the side of the road and preparations were made for a picnic. It was a fine and sunny spring day, so we could sit on the grass, although some of us preferred to put coats down first. There was plenty of space between the hedgerows and the road and no traffic. Everybody tucked in and ate up most of the food we had brought – sandwiches and cake, with maybe an apple or orange to follow. Those who were not content with spring water had brought bottles of spruce or flavoured juice.

The picnics then were very special. We all joined in the clear up. No rubbish was left behind. Children, with a sudden burst of energy after eating, wanted to climb into the nearby wood and see what they could find. The adults, in no hurry to move, agreed we could go for a while. But Grandma gave us strict instructions not to tear up masses of bluebells from their roots. That would damage their bulbs. In any case, we had plenty to carry without a huge arm-full of bluebells, primroses, cowslips and anemones (we called these 'enemies'). We were beginning to find all kinds of interesting things when we were called back and everybody had to set off again along the road.

At that time, the road was little more than a track. Grass grew in the middle. Rough and narrow widths of tarmac were there to carry the weight of cartwheels and stopped carts getting stuck in the mud. This road continued along the Welland valley, towards Market Harborough, and only began to improve as we approached the main town of the area. The road back seemed endless, but there were now more familiar villages ahead and soon we would be near Bram Wood.

Uncle Harry knew a short cut across the fields which would get us back home more quickly, so we climbed a stile leading to a farm we knew and cut the busy corner on Harborough Road to emerge quite near to the railway bridge on the outskirts of Desborough. Arthur and I could then race ahead and get home before the others.

We passed the station and continued down Station Road, happily waving to the rest as we went in the opposite direction. Elsie and her family left down Queen Street. Arthur and I ran on to wait on the doorstep of number 4 Regent Street. Grandad arrived some time later, produced the back door key and let us in. We sat down inside and waited to get our breath back. It had been quite a day!

The Butcher's

Grandma had learned she could trust me to carry out any errand she sent me on, whatever it was, loaves from the baker's, hot ready-to-eat dinners from that new and enterprising shop, which had started providing a valuable and popular service near the butcher's. Occasionally, Grandma would want a few extra vegetables from the greengrocer's, but nearly always there was meat from the butcher's to collect. I could be relied on to bring back exactly what she wanted and the correct change.

On Fridays, partly because Friday was the traditional day, partly because she needed a change from always cooking for the family, it was fish and chips. Two pen'orth of fish and a pen'orth of chips for each of us.

'But, be sure to go to Haycock's, not that other shop down by the Town Cross. Haycock's is always the best,' she would assure me.

Sometimes, I got there early, before they had started frying. The oil was not yet hot enough for the prepared fish and chips to be slithered in. To pass the time, I would go round Tailby's the butcher, and peer in through the bars of the slaughterhouse. Earlier that day, some of us boys had, probably, helped the men make sure the animals being taken there were driven, with sticks, into the side road. There the slaughterhouse had been built adjoining the shop in the main Station Road.

Sometimes, they arrived by wagon and the tail-piece of the cart had to be let down and animals packed inside driven into a cow-shed or sheep-pen to wait their turn for slaughter. Pigs, no doubt, sensing trouble ahead, made most noise. I can't remember any goats. Our area was not hilly enough. If there were any kept by their owners for milk and cheese, they were valued too highly for slaughter.

The men tended to deal with bulls and bullocks first. Bulls were especially dangerous and would pin anyone unused to the job against the slaughterhouse wall, if given the chance. If the bull was exceptionally large and dangerous, he would be driven or pulled through the ring in his nose, straight into the slaughterhouse. This monstrous mountain of muscle came snorting in, looking for anyone who was trying to restrict his behaviour. Immediately, the skilled executioner would lift his pole-axe and drive it through the skull of this monster. The weight and speed of the animal simply meant the axe went into his skull more deeply.

Amazingly, the bull crumbled instantly and sank to the floor, bleeding profusely, soon to be converted into a huge carcass of meat and bones. The men, as they paused to breathe again, would see us peering through the grill on the outside wall and shout at us to bugger off. Obligingly, we would pretend to comply, only to return as soon as more animals were driven in.

Later, a group of sad, compliant sheep came bundling in, looking mournfully to see possible exits. Appealing eyes got them nowhere. There was no question of a fight for freedom. They continued to baa in chorus until they had all taken their turn to be made into raw meat. Pigs seemed to increase their noise as their throats were cut. I'd swear they still managed to scream, even after dispatch. They seemed to be demanding that the job be finished properly, even as they were thrown into huge tanks of boiling water.

For us boys, it was, of course, a good deal more exciting than queuing up for fish and chips. But I had been sent for some and all the family were relying on me. The errand had to be completed.

Slaughtering animals was quite the usual way to make sure butchers were supplied. But the best butchers were always careful to prepare the meat for sale in a back room off the shop. Any unwanted bone would be removed and splinters of bone were never allowed to get into the enjoyment of eating fresh meat.

Grandma did not buy from Tailby's, but from another butcher, Kilborn's, whom we reached first when we set off along Station Road to the shops. Kilborn's was, probably, slightly more high-class. Everything was spick and span, and the meat presented attractively, so that any shopper could make the choice she wanted. Trays of chops, legs, steaks, shin of beef, liver were all there – everything anybody could wish for.

There was no slaughterhouse behind the shop and no way, I could see, where animals could be driven in. The shoppers had no need to think about those problems. It was regarded as no concern of theirs. Abattoirs were later built in areas some distance away and many more animals were then dealt with together. Who was it who thought it a good idea to adopt a French word, instead of slaughterhouses?

Dr Gerald

The family belonged to the doctor's club and paid a small weekly subscription to get treatment when needed. When I was a child, there were two doctors at the Harborough Road surgery. Old Dr Gibbons and his son, Dr Gerald, who had had the benefit of longer training and could, when needed, perform minor operations in a patient's home.

I went through the usual range of minor difficulties when I was still quite young – chickenpox (but very little) and measles rather badly. At that time, doctors believed that measles had to be dealt with carefully and curtains in my bedroom were pulled to shut out the light. Otherwise, my eyesight might have been affected. There were various alarms about scarlet fever and even smallpox. One young man we knew had to be put in a specially got-together bedroom in the Council hut in the Rec. He was there for weeks, until the signs of the disease had disappeared. We could peer through the curtains there to see if he was still living.

My main affliction was tonsillitis, which recurred time and again. Finally, Dr Gerald advised that he should carry out a minor operation to remove my tonsils. At the same time, it would be as well to remove adenoids from my nasal passages. Otherwise they, too, would also be causing trouble.

Mother agreed and the fatal day dawned. I was to remain in bed in my nightclothes, whilst the bedroom was converted into an operating theatre. I was to lie on a table, which first had to be carried from the kitchen (the only place with a suitable small table which was easy to move) up to the bedroom. The kitchen was dark and hardly the place in which to operate. The bedroom was light and had two windows at the front and one at the back. Mother and Grandma made the table as comfortable as possible for me to lie on, with a clean sheet uppermost.

Soon, Dr Gerald arrived with his large black bag, full of surgical instruments, and accompanied by a nurse who got everything ready, both on the bed and at the side, where Dr Gerald's fearsome-looking instruments were arranged. I then had to climb onto the table and be tucked tightly in, so there would be no danger of my falling off. My head and shoulders were left exposed, but protective material fixed around my neck and shoulders, where there was likely to be blood spilt.

When Dr Gerald had been suitably dressed in his surgeon's gear, his mouth and nose covered with special care, he declared we could begin. After a brief explanation to me of what was going to happen, I had to prepare myself for unconsciousness, so that I would not have to suffer awareness of what Dr Gerald was about to do. The nurse, fully dressed also for the operation, came by my side and told me she was going to put a cover over my nose and mouth. I was to just breathe normally until I went to sleep. I couldn't see what it was they were giving me to put me out, but there was some form of gas cylinder by the side of the table, from which the gas was released. I soon became unconscious and maybe dreamt.

When I woke up, Dr Gerald was about to leave, having been restored to his usual suit and spectacles. I felt my mouth, which was very sore and still bleeding. My nose didn't feel too good either. Dr Gerald assured me I would soon be fine. It would hurt for a bit, but I would soon be able to breathe better and not suffer any more tonsillitis. No more tonsillitis, just sore throats and blocked nasal passages, I found, long after my throat and nose had more or less recovered. All this was carried out upstairs, where there was no hot water. A lot of boiling water must have been needed throughout the operation and all of it had to be carried upstairs in large jugs. Aunt Doris had such a jug full of hot water, which she used for washing before going to work at the wholesale factory.

It is, perhaps, just as well that that operation, with all its risks, has gone out of fashion. Hospitals aim to be more hygienic and take great care to ensure safe and successful operations. Nurses are just as sympathetic and caring as they always were. I felt then, as now, I could trust them to look after me like a son. Doctors and surgeons still have the appearance and assumption of superiority, which any magician has decorated himself in over the ages. Having performed their magic rites, they disappear in a cloud of smoke.

Sunday School Anniversaries

One of the year's events we looked forward to was the celebration of the Sunday School Anniversary. This was in July but we spent weeks preparing for it. Special hymns were selected and we had to learn them.

Sunday School was, normally, on Sunday afternoons and we were divided into groups of boys and girls according to ages and we all had our own special teacher. Mine was a coalman during the week, but on Sundays he was all spruced up and took his teaching very seriously. He had been in the First World War in Palestine and had suffered injuries to his face and jaw. He was writing a diary of his experiences there. After we had gone through a period of bible study, based on the text for the day, he would read extracts from his diary. They proved very exciting, but we couldn't really understand why he, quite a mild man, should be out in this hot, dry Middle Eastern country, fighting people called Turks, who were used to living there and who were said to be threatening neighbouring countries, not at all like England.

After Sunday School, we gathered in the church, boys properly dressed and girls with new dresses for the occasion. The parson would introduce the hymns, which we enjoyed and sang vigorously. But then, we sank back in our seats and waited, whilst the parson gave the customary sermon. We accepted that it was something which had to be gone through, to qualify for what we were really looking forward to, on the next day.

Monday was Sports Day on the Rec. All the teachers were there and my teacher was in charge of events – the order of races, who was to run in each and who held the finishing tape and decided on the first three in each race. It all began with flat races – probably a roughly measured distance, perhaps 80 strides, rather than a carefully measured 100 yards. The winners were given tickets to go and claim their prizes, some modest amount of cash. More interesting races followed – the sack race with several of the competitors falling over as they got their feet tangled up in the sack as they ran, the 3-legged race (a pair who linked up and had their middle ankles tied together by tape) with more tumbles, and of course, the egg and spoon race (pot eggs carried in spoons, liable to drop them at every bump).

The races concluded when the charabancs arrived to take us out into the countryside. These early buses were most impressive and it was a great treat to have a ride in them. They, no doubt, began as long carts, pulled by a pair of horses, but the charabancs I remember were, no doubt, an improvement on those. Now covered in, steps up at the back and seats down the two sides, with windows to look out of. The wheels were covered with solid rubber tyres, because the pneumatic tyre had not yet been invented. The engine chugged away, rather noisily, under a flat bonnet and the driver set off cautiously, watching out for pot-holes in the roughly made roads. It was all very different and exciting, as far as we were concerned.

We passed round the Back Lanes to Bram Wood. In the spring, this was covered with bluebells, primroses and cowslips and was a real haven for wildlife. At the corner of the Wood that we passed there was a pond, under the trees, where, we learnt from the keeper, foxes and other wild animals came to drink at night. After Bram Wood, we set off along the river Welland valley making for Rockingham Castle. The villages still had their attractive thatched cottages, with red sandstone walls. Rockingham Castle was built of similar stone and sat solidly at the top of a steep hill, looking down over the valley. It was open for special parties, who could enjoy afternoon tea on the terrace outside.

We enjoyed that, and afterwards, we were free to go in search of small presents or an ice-cream to buy with our sports price-money.

These outings were over too quickly, but we could continue the celebration going home in the bus, by singing popular songs together:

'In Dublin's fair city where the girls are so pretty
I first set my eyes on sweet Molly Malone
As she wheeled her wheelbarrow through streets broad and narrow
Crying cockles and mussels, alive, alive-o!'

or

'Oh Danny boy, the pipes, the pipes are calling
From glen to glen and down the mountain side.'

Maybe some of the boys would think this too sentimental and would start something else in competition:

'Old Macdonald had a farm
Ee-ay, ee-ay, oh!
And on that farm he kept some cows
Ee-ay, ee-ay, oh!
With a moo-moo here, and a moo-moo there
Here a moo, there a moo, everywhere a moo-moo.'

They made the most of the animal noises, passing swiftly from sheep to bulls and finally to pigs:

Here an oi, there an oi, everywhere an oi-oi!'

The loud, guttural noises meant to imitate pigs sounding annoyed, soon blotted out the quieter songs and always ended in peals of laughter.

Neither the teachers who had accompanied us, nor the driver seemed to mind. They, too, had been young once and liked to see children enjoying themselves.

We arrived all too soon back at the Rec. and saying good-bye to our friends and the teachers, set off home. Everybody agreed we had had a really good day. The local schools had cooperated too and given us a day's holiday, but next day, it was back to school again. Life is like that. You cannot expect sugar on the cake all the time!

The Hospital Fête

Our Sunday School Anniversary was arranged for everybody belonging to the Congregational Church. A much bigger celebration, in which the whole town took part, came later in the summer – the Hospital Fête.

In those days, there was no National Health Service. Hospitals had to rely on voluntary contributions and legacies. Ordinary working people mostly paid regularly into the Hospital Saturday Fund. Their subscriptions ensured that the Fund paid the cost of any stay in hospital, including doctors and specialists brought in from elsewhere. The wealthy could support the rest of the community by paying large sums for all or part of a local hospital to be built. Their name would then be given to a new extension or be placed prominently at the entrance to a new ward. Apart from this individual funding, every town in the area arranged a Hospital Fête, making it lavish enough to outdo neighbouring towns. The big question every town faced, annually, was how could they provide the best street entertainment and raise record sums of money to give to their local hospital.

A local committee was given the task of organizing the Fête and they had to meet for intensive discussions early in the year, long before the Saturday, set aside in July, when the Fête would take place. We got the first inkling of what the committee had planned, when posters appeared all over the town, in shop windows, in the Council Offices and on every lamp post. Competitions were listed on the posters – football matches between local teams, races for children and more professional athletes. Major attractions were to be brought in from further afield – a polo match and even motorbike races. All this would take place on the Football Ground, where there was plenty of space. There were to be stalls of food, flowers and handicrafts, with the main area of activity roped off, in front of the football stand.

Very soon, the whole town was buzzing. Pubs, Working Men's and Conservative Clubs, factories, the Co-op and lots of smaller organizations met to decide what each could enter. Most of them wanted to join the procession round the town, which marked the beginning of the celebrations. This involved providing their own decorated dray, pulled by a horse, not an easy beginning for those without farming connections. But every dray was expected to display a magnificent tableau, advertising the organization's aims and above this, build a super-structure loaded with flowers, such as to provoke a chorus of 'Ooh, aahs!'

The Old Stone Cross.

Somehow a special message had to be got across.

The day of the Fête finally arrived. People packed the route: Station Road, Rushton Road, Union Street, Victoria Street, High Street, Gold Street, Braybrook Road, right up to the Football Ground. Where there seemed to be no more space on the pavements, people appeared in the top windows of houses en route and waved to those below. We knew the procession had started when we heard the Mission Band start playing and gradually get nearer. Everybody cheered as the Band passed by, followed by the decorated drays, on which actors provided entertainment. In front and at the side, were clowns up to all kinds of antics, holding out long poles with bags hanging from the end, which were designed to reach top windows of houses at the side and to encourage watchers there to drop money into the bag. The clowns did not miss much.

By the time that section of the procession had passed, a second surprise was in store. Appearing round the distant corner, came the Albion Band, intent on attracting even more attention than its Rowell rival, the leaders. A further group of decorated drays followed and the end of the procession was marked by a group of ambulance men and police.

Everybody now followed as fast as they could to the Football Ground, where the judges, who had earlier inspected the displays, had retired to the football dressing-room to choose the best and most original entry and award the 1st prize. Meantime, the children could ride on ponies or bump around the field in horse-drawn brakes. The stalls were already doing a roaring trade, not to men-

Desborough Church.

Regent Street.

tion the ice-cream salesmen from Italy.

All this was brought to a halt, when the polo teams appeared on their horses and began cantering around the pitch provided for them. The match provided a new excitement for Desborough. Some preferred it to motorbikes racing each other in circuits later on. All the same, we noticed that more police and ambulance men stood at the ropes and kept people safely back, just in case of accidents.

The most spectacular event of the evening, which had people staring skywards, was the arrival of an RAF bi-plane overhead. After hovering, almost motionless above, it began to dive and loop-the-loop, skimming the heads of the crowd below, before zooming back skywards again. Not satisfied with that, the pilot then switched his engine off and seemed to be falling out-of-control, twisting and turning like a falling leaf. At the last minute, close to the ground, the pilot re-started his engine, flew swiftly upwards and quickly left in the direction of his home-station, just as though it was nothing spectacular. All in the day's work.

There were still plenty of attractions on the ground to keep the crowd spending for the benefit of the Hospital. No doubt a dance in the wooden hut, which provided space for such activities. The band was already tuning up, when the time came for us to leave. Children were not expected to stay up for 'lights out'. They had had a good time and now could wind down a little and prepare for bed. It was, after all, Sunday next day.

Collecting the Rents

The Dawkins Builders, who had constructed many of the streets and houses in our part of Desborough, was managed by my Grandad's father, Grandad and Grandad's brother Joseph. Fortunately for us, they had the forethought to build homes for themselves and the families to follow. Joseph was also an undertaker and it was always a bit of a strange experience for me to be taken down a step into the house at the end of Victoria Street and perhaps go through to the workshop, where coffins were being made. Joseph had two sons, Alf and Harold, strapping lads already hard at work, measuring, planing and finishing off with brassware to suit the customer's wishes. There was also a very nice sister, Nellie, who, immediately made a great fuss of me and invited us to have a cup of tea with her in the back room. She would be there in the church pew behind us on Sundays. I could tell she was one of us.

In addition to the big house we lived in, Grandad owned six in Queen Street. Queen Street ran parallel to Regent Street and the top end of the gardens of the six houses met the fence round our orchard. Three of these houses were slightly superior to the others and had bay windows. They were in a terrace and were approached either directly through a small front garden to the front door, or through an entry built between two of the houses, with bedrooms above. In the lowest one of the three, number 17, my Father and Mother had started their married life and my brother, Arthur, was born there. Next door, at number 15, the Tebbutts lived, a slightly 'stand-offish' couple, with a much-prized daughter, Hilda, who seemed most of the time to be hidden away. Mrs Tebbutt, and sometimes Hilda, did, however, appear at the Chapel on Sundays. Round the corner of this house was number 13, the Burton's. This was a slightly depressed house. Mrs Burton always made me welcome, but she had lost her husband. The mainstay of the family was Jimmy, who worked for the Ironstone Company, a tough cheery young man, but, in such a job, unlucky enough to suffer injuries from time to time.

Jimmy used to help Grandad around the house and garden on his days off and I remember with admiration one job he tackled that took weeks to complete. Our water, at that time, came partly from an underground spring, which had been made into a large, brick well, which was, occasionally, damaged by bad weather. There was a tall pump, enclosed by a wooden frame an attached to the outside wall of the house near the kitchen and back entrance. A large metal handle at the side pumped the water up from the well, which was sited in the middle of a piece of garden, immediately outside the house. It was not simply a question of the pump mechanism going wrong. There were problems in the well underground. Jimmy Burton arrived to see what he could find and began digging the earth away and piling it to the sides. He was so experienced at digging, he soon began to disappear below, until he finally revealed the well. In fact, some of the brickwork had collapsed and was preventing water being pumped up. Instead, it was trying to get out elsewhere.

I had to admire the strength and vigour of Jimmy, the skilled manual worker, sweating profusely, but quite sure he could master the problem in the end. Eventually, he did, of course. He restored the carefully constructed walls of the well, following the usual curves in the brick-work, learned by generations of underground builders of walls and culverts. He had to rely on good weather to prepare the mortar and fix the bricks with it below. I could have raised quite a cheer (much as builders do when they complete a chimney on a roof-top and decorate it with a fir-tree) when Jimmy finally fixed the top back on the well and asked Grandad, stationed above ground, to try it. The pump now worked perfectly and we could fill any number of buckets of water to use in the garden.

Jimmy and Grandad sat down nearby to enjoy a cup of tea, a sure sign that a good job had been completed. Maybe Jimmy would have preferred something stronger in a glass, but all our family were then teetotallers. After that, Jimmy and I were firm friends and he would, occasionally, take me to the Ironstone pits and show me things most outsiders knew nothing about.

My family had left number 17 Queen Street by then, following my Father's death in 1918. We now lived with our grandparents. Aunt Elsie and Uncle Fred were then able to move in from Rowell and have a home of their own. Up till then, they had lived with Fred's family in Rowell. I never collected Aunt Elsie's rent. Presumably, if any was paid to her parents, she brought it over herself on her frequent visits.

The other three terraced houses were further down Queen Street and rent was a bit lower. When I started to collect the rents for Grandma, the rent was 1/2d a week, instead of 1/6d for the three further up the street. But these houses were smaller and had no bay windows. All the houses had well kept gardens and some huts at the top end abutting buildings on our side. Some had even built a small building there – perhaps a place to keep birds or rabbits, even flowers in some cases. They were all homes to be valued.

One was occupied by a grown-up family, the Panters, which always seemed too packed for me to go in. I had to wait at the door for somebody to pay the rent. Another house was occupied by a relation of some kind, also named Dawkins. The lowest one sheltered a rather lonely lady, known as Mary Jane. Probably her surname, like so many Desborians, was Coe.

She was a friendly old soul, who always invited me in. Being on her own and far from well, she loved 'a bit of company.' She would offer me a cup of tea, but I politely declined. I had other rents to collect, after all. That made little difference. She simply ignored the possibility of me leaving and went on to tell me all about her ailments, a favourite subject of hers. She had seen the doctor, having suffered severe pain in her side and lower regions. He had called regularly, but had been unable to offer much help, merely painkillers. Then, to my amazement she produced a bag of little stones and showed them to me. I had no idea what they were. They just looked like any small stones I might pick up in the gutter.

'Gallstones!' she explained and started to pummel her middle and lower regions. 'Found them in the pot when I was tipping it outside every morning!' It still didn't mean a lot. I was blissfully unaware at that time of how my innards worked. So far as I was concerned, they ticked over smoothly every day, so there was nothing to worry about. I simply enjoyed regular meals at home and kept 'regular' as they used to say.

How on earth did anybody collect stones internally? Surely anything that came out of the garden was well washed and cooked before eating. Any grit or dust was carefully removed. Was it, simply, that Mary Jane put anything and everything down her throat and hoped for the best?

It was certainly a lesson for me to watch what I ate. I found myself feeling my stomach and looking surreptitiously at my outgoings. Not to my liking at all. However, I got 6d a week for collecting the rents. Grandma appreciated the help and I intended to continue. I had to learn to treat each tenant differently, and with care. I would soon be in trouble if I simply turned up to grab the money and leave.

There were problems, sometimes, to do with every house. After a particularly severe storm, slates might be lost, roofs were letting in the rain. Grandad, being the landlord, was expected to get a builder in to put things right. Later on, I wondered how he could do it out of so low a rent. It didn't seem to matter. He had the houses kept in good order, on the principle that it was better to spend a little now, than have to foot a heavy bill later. Years later, when Grandma was left on her own and had no husband or builder at hand to look after the cottages, she decided to sell them to sitting tenants. I think she got £150 for the smaller houses and £250 for the better ones. It seemed little recompense in her old age for looking after her tenants so well.

The irony of the situation was emphasized when some of the tenants later sold the houses for a much higher price and left to live elsewhere in a bigger house than they had been used to.

The sale of the houses came many years after I had been rent collector for Grandma. As a child, I had always been close to her and I treasured that relationship. There were many things we did together, which I remember vividly. Simple childish things I really enjoyed. Often she would invite me to come and help her make the Yorkshire pudding for Sunday's roast. I had to stir the mixture thoroughly, which she had prepared in a large light brown pot bowl. All the lumps had to be smoothed out. They would show up badly when Grandma finally poured the liquid round the large hunk of beef, already roasted in the middle of the pan. The meat gravy smelt really inviting. I could hardly wait. Yorkshire pudding was always served as a separate first course. Well risen, but also solid enough to satisfy hungry children. We had no doubt, the Sunday roast was the best meal of the week.

On other days, Grandma would let me help her prepare a cake mixture or sweet pudding. The best part of that was being allowed to lick the remnants still left in the basin. 'A taste of honey' almost. Certainly, I removed every scrap still sticking to the basin with my forefinger, which I licked again and again. Grandma simply told me not to smack my lips so loudly.

I was definitely a favoured child, to some extent taking the place of Doris, Grandma's youngest, who was now getting quite grown up. Doris had, unfortunately, suffered a serious thyroid operation on her neck and had spent weeks away from home in a Convalescent Home. She was now regarded as a delicate child, not strong enough to continue working at the Corset Factory, but maintaining her independence by becoming a full-time piano teacher. Naturally, there was some rivalry between Doris and me for Grandma's attention. Somehow, Grandma managed it all very well and left us both with a feeling that we were much loved.

Grandma lived modestly in her old age. Always the gracious lady, careful to wear a clean crocheted front every day, above an equally carefully chosen dress. She was respected by her neighbours and much valued, over the years, for her contribution to the Mother's Weekly Meeting held in the Sunday School. It was largely a social occasion for Grandma and her contemporaries. As she got older, she began to suffer more illness and was confined to bed for a time, by the doctor. I used to go back home, as soon as possible, to see how she was. She expected me to make her smile and pull herself together again. She always said I was as good as any tonic and went on living contentedly with her remaining family till she was 89.

A Bike Ride

My brother Arthur and cousin Howard were getting to the age when boys decide to venture further from the nest. Both of them celebrated a common birthday, 15 April, with Howard a year younger. Howard had been given a spanking new bike for his birthday. A Raleigh, from Burditt's, our local supplier, with a 3-speed, a new gadget almost unknown in our area. Being an only child, Howard always got what he wanted. Parents and grandparents on his father's side were willing to indulge this only boy of the Rains family and the one intended to carry on the Rains dynasty. Arthur was not as lucky. He, no doubt, got small presents he wanted, but, as far as a bike was concerned, he had to be content with borrowing Doris' bike, a ladies' bike with no crossbar, otherwise, at a pinch, I could have sat there. Naturally, Howard would not risk even a scratch on his prized possession, let alone have me on the crossbar, sitting on the 3-speed. As far as he was concerned, it was all important to have the 3-speed readily accessible. He could then display how to change down for uphills and change up for easy descents.

Arthur and Howard had been planning a day's bike ride since 15 April. Their intention was to go north, towards Rockingham Castle, and Uppingham, where there was a well-known public school they were curious to see. There they would turn right and make a circuit returning via Kettering, where Arthur had started at the Grammar School. It was an ambitious undertaking and they could not be lumbered with me. In any case, I had no bike.

Not to be outdone, I came up with the proposal that I should ride Dad's old full-sized bike. It seemed, at first, a ridiculous proposal. If I sat on the saddle, my feet would be dangling, nowhere near the pedals. The only way I could ride it, was to put my right foot through to the other pedal, underneath the crossbar. By grasping the handlebars firmly and pushing most of my weight on the left foot, I demonstrated that I could ride the bike.

'You'll never keep up with us. We are going a long way!' was Arthur's rejoinder.

'How on earth will we get home if you fall off and have a crash?' said Howard, 'It's a silly idea!'

I persisted and got more competent at my circus-like contortions, which surprised them both.

'Hmm.' said Howard, 'Maybe we'll let you come, but don't expect us to go at your pace all the time!'

My next obstacle was persuading Mam to let me go. It would last all day, in any case, and we would need sandwiches. After pointing out all the problems I was likely to meet, she agreed reluctantly, provided Arthur would let me take Doris' ladies' bike occasionally, and he ride the full-sized bike to give me a rest.

The great day came and we set out towards Stoke Albany. This was easy going to begin with. Mam had insisted that we should stick to the quiet, country roads, where there was very little traffic. All the same, I still soon fell behind.

'I told you not to come!' shouted Arthur, 'We haven't even started to climb hills yet! Here, take this bike. It gets more difficult before we reach Cottingham.'

Reluctantly, I agreed and after a brief pause to catch my breath, we set off again uphill, but travelling now more in a bunch.

The woods looked glorious with all their spring flowers, bluebells, primroses, cowslips and violets. Trees were already out in leaf. The thought did occur to me, it would be more sensible to drop out now and let the other two speed ahead. That would have been shameful. If they could complete this round-ride, so could I.

Just to confound me and my determination to keep going, Howard and Arthur soon stopped on the side of the road and dropped their bikes, underneath an impressive row of horse chestnuts. They kicked the fallen crop of conkers, which had survived since the previous autumn, and started to pick up some beauties. This particular tree had, no doubt, been chosen and carefully planted there by local gentry. The mansion, where they lived, could be seen standing well back from the road and partially hidden by more trees and bushes. Howard soon filled his new saddle-bag, in with the bike tools, whilst Arthur and I put some in our pockets.

We were then ready to set off again. It was now a flat road along the Welland valley and Arthur, almost absent-mindedly, took the ladies' bike. I resumed my contortions behind. Rockingham Castle soon appeared in sight, looking glorious, as its brown sandstone shone in the sun. Woods around the castle gave us another excuse (good for me, anyway) to stop and look over the wall at the special-looking deer, which were kept there. The fawns were light brown in colour. The stags, clearly identified by their huge antlers, were a much darker brown. As soon as we were spotted looking over the wall, the deer took fright and bolted further into the trees.

The deer matched the colour of all the cottages we passed by. The villages with cottages grouped together consisted of a main street, mostly of individual homesteads, with thatched roofs. Occasionally, they were being repaired by thatchers, who paused from the rooftops to shout down encouragement to three assorted cyclists passing by.

'Go on tich!' one cried out, 'Show 'em you can leave them standing.' He had, at once, spotted that some kind of racing competition was going on between us and thought it only right to support the youngest and smallest at the back.

We might have expected more deer to look at us through gaps between the houses, but met only a carthorse pulling a dray through the High Street. It slowed us up a bit.

'Keep going, young 'un!' cried the driver encouragingly. I put on a special spurt for the spectators.

We soon got to Oakham, as far north as we intended to go. Its main feature, the public school on the crossroads. Walls at the back seemed clearly designed to keep out nosey-parkers. Again, built of brown and red sandstone, but more carefully cut and carefully laid to fit. Cottages left room between rough stones to allow a bird or mouse to build in them. There was plenty of space around the school for more buildings, if there was a need to expand. We had passed a wide entrance, as we came up the hill, which led to sports fields, carefully marked for a variety of sports. For the first time, I realized that two high posts with a crossbar between them meant rugby was played there, although I learnt more about that curious sport when I, later, went to Kettering Grammar School and had my trials for scrum half or wing three-quarters. Soccer had been bred into me much earlier and that continued to be my preferred game. Rugby was surely designed by a rather clever mathematician for the toffs. Soccer was for the working class. When playing rugby, the players could handle the ball, curiously oval in shape, but when they had scored beneath the posts (sorry, made a try), they had to convert the try. The ball had to be kicked from a spot, carefully measured some distance away. If the player succeeded in sending it over the crossbar, the team were awarded more points. In soccer, only the goal-keeper could handle the ball. I learned later that foreigners thought the rules for cricket were just as curious. But I had seen and heard that being played in the Water Works field on Harrington Road, so cricket seemed quite normal to me.

Having satisfied our curiosity, we turned right in front of the school and started to pedal along a main road. More traffic meant special care had to be taken. I feared that, with my unorthodox way of riding a bike, I might be stopped by a policeman and told to walk. It was quite a relief to turn right again in the direction of Rockingham Forest, Weldon and Geddington. Near the forest, we all agreed it was time to stop and eat our sandwiches. Howard was lucky enough to have a bottle of spruce to drink. He generously let Arthur and me have a quick swallow. We had brought no drink and hoped to find a village tap to satisfy our thirst.

Refreshed, we set off again through Geddington, in the direction of Kettering. Howard had the great idea of making for Wicksteed's Park, set up by a local benefactor, and a great attraction for miles around. There was a large lake with rowboats. Sometimes there were races between pairs of them, a cox facing towards the finishing post and the crew of skilled oarsmen facing the opposite direction and matching their strokes to the man in front. The speed of these long, narrow boats made me whistle. They would have left me on my mother's bike far behind in any race. There were paddleboats near a large pavilion, which could be rented for 20 minutes at a time. Most of that time seemed to be spent in bumping other boats and trying to get out of a tangle to return to the quay-side.

Howard thought it would be unwise to leave the bikes unattended, whilst they went inside the pavilion to find an ice-cream. The responsible job of guard duty was, of course, given to me. I did get a lick of the over-flowing ice-creams Howard and Arthur came back with. That had to serve as my reward.

It was already getting late and as we left, progress was noticeably slower. Going down hill towards the centre of Kettering was easy enough. Climbing the hill on the other side was much slower. Howard assured us this was the shortest route, so we soldiered on, past the Workhouse, the Cattle Market and the Grammar School, making for Rushton. We were not used to crossing a big town like Kettering, but with great caution, we got through and onto the country roads at last.

Over to our left, below, we could see the railway, which was not far from Rushton and Desborough – an encouraging thought. Kettering brickworks, with its high chimney belching out smoke, stood out as we passed. The road was reasonably straightforward after that, over the railway and then dropping down to Rushton. We passed the milestone near Rushton Hall and then the Triangular Lodge, appealing as ever and keen to tempt us in. It began to look like familiar territory. We raised a muted cheer as we dropped down to Harry Cook's Lodge, but saved our breath to climb the hill past the cemetery. At that point, I had had enough. The wide space, gravelled in front of the heavy cemetery gates, was a place for anybody and everybody to rest a while, before deciding they were bound for the peace inside or the final quiet departure homewards. I decided to walk the rest of the way, leaving Howard and Arthur to race ahead and see who could get home first.

My right leg was very tired and inclined to develop cramp. My left leg felt ready to crumble, even when I was walking slowly. Certainly to walk at my own pace was far better than trying to keep up with the other mad pair.

Needless to say, when they arrived at 4 Regent Street, Mam and Grandma were very concerned to see I was not with them.

'What have you done with Trevor? Is he alright?' they both asked.

'He's just coming,' Howard assured them, and then, tactfully, disappeared to his home in Queen Street, leaving Arthur to take the dressing-down to follow. When, finally, I dragged my heels and the heavy

bike round the corner and home, I was embraced by both Mam and Grandma, and both of us were taken in for a tea specially prepared for us. It was almost worth all that effort, not something I would easily forget.

Howard told me later we had covered 50 miles and not many kids with an old bike like mine could manage such a distance. I think I felt as tired as Dick Whittington when he and his cat, finally, arrived above London and searched for those pavements of gold.

I felt I could puff out my chest a bit to friends of my age, who had never even ventured as far as Pipewell Woods. Now that was a place, a bit nearer, we could visit next time. Meantime, I wondered how to get a bike I could reach. Maybe a Raleigh?

The Arrival of the Cinema

At the bottom of Station Road, opposite the back of the George Inn and the yard above, where my Sunday School teacher lived, was the Oddfellows Hall. In that area, I often met Harry Crick, the Sunday School teacher, who was also a coal man, delivering sacks of fuel to local houses, during the week. In that part of Desborough, too, was a sweet shop I liked to visit and our dentist, whom I visited more reluctantly. Mam took me to see him, when I was soon to take up my scholarship place at Kettering Grammar. Mr Shand turned out to be a very nice and careful man, not hell-bent on whipping a tooth out, if it showed any signs of decay. Unfortunately, he found that I had not looked after my teeth as I should have done. He suggested I should eat fewer sweets and then set about stopping further decay. I was reminded of that upstairs surgery every time I came to find out what was on next week at the Oddfellows Hall.

This was one of the biggest Halls in Desborough. It had been regularly used for shows and meetings of all kinds. The Oddfellows had been set up as a friendly society, the object to help workers who were sick or unable to work. Members paid a small amount weekly and could claim benefit, when left without wages. The secretary of the Oddfellows was Charlie Groocock, who lived just round the corner near us. He was distantly related to the Bosworths, our friends next door to us in Regent Street.

There were regular meetings of the Oddfellows Committee, but, some time ago, they had been approached to allow film projectors to be brought in to show some of the early films imported from America. Eventually, the Hall was sold to a new company distributing these films. The Hall was then given the name of The Ritz. This was during the early 1920s, when some of the outstanding early silent films were being shown. I loved Charlie Chaplin right from the start. He had begun life in the Elephant and Castle in the centre of London, but carried a bit of old England with him when he moved to Hollywood. Poor Charlie, always in trouble, always making us laugh with his antics, his boots, bowler hat and stick, somehow too big for him. Laurel and Hardy followed. Laurel was always pulling faces and looking miserable and near to tears, until he had persuaded Hardy to go his way into trouble. Buster Keaton was another, A long-faced and unsmiling comedian. They all made it a real treat to attend the children's matinees for 3d a time (adults 6d).

We used to sit at the front of the hall, if possible, on long, wooden bench seats, cracking monkey-nuts, eating sweets noisily and impatient for the show to begin. The projector was high up behind us, throwing a beam of light on the large canvas screen mounted on the platform in front of us. First the film was wound on spools, tested for quality and no breaks and then focused on the screen, care being taken to ensure the picture sat squarely and could be seen clearly, its captions underneath. When a well-known local pianist appeared at the grand piano, placed at the side of the screen, we knew the film would soon start.

The pianist was in no hurry and first took sheets of music out of his case, checked that the piano was in tune and improvised a bit, to loosen up his fingers. He then began an overture of some kind, chosen to suit the mood of the film to follow. If it was a Wild West film, there would be galloping horses and rumbles of an exciting encounter between Cowboys and Red Indians. The music matched the film and stirred up the climax, as battle commenced on the screen. There were sad, sentimental stories of families living in poverty or of some poor woman out singing in the snow, hoping, in vain, that someone in those cosy, but firmly closed, houses would take pity on her. Perhaps even invite her in beside a glowing fire or, at least, offer something charitable to help her on her way. This was, after all, an echo of the current popularity of Charles Dickens.

Things had to change when, in the late 1920s, talkie films began to oust the silent ones. To begin with, the live pianist, who had added so much to earlier films, was no longer required. The talkie provided a much squeakier accompaniment and sometimes, sound got out of phase with the picture and caused much raucous laughter. Then films got better and we had the Marx Brothers, fresh from vaudeville, with Groucho of the moustache and funny walk, full of all kinds of antics, making up to Mrs Ponsonby or opening a small cupboard on board ship to reveal dozens of stowaways falling out on to the deck. Chico, with the dumb Harpo his accomplice at the piano, would try to tell a story or to sing, but be prevented from going on by inconsequential noise and skilful hand manoeuvres by Harpo at the piano. Not quite the same thing as our silent film pianist had to offer, but very funny just the same. Cartoon films from Disneyland, like Felix the Cat, Leo the Lion or the seven dwarfs did not have the same appeal for me.

As an alternative to this film entertainment, we were fortunate enough to have a Music Hall set up in the old Baptist Chapel, which was sold like the Oddfellows Hall, when no longer needed. This building had been partially reconstructed, mainly inside, but there was a ramp round the outside to provide another entrance for those wishing to sit in the 'Gods' – paying rather more than in the cinema – 4d for children! The great attractions heading the bill were usually well-known stand-up comics, along Flanagan and Allen lines, from the West End. They were backed up by singers and instrumental performers, who varied quite a lot in quality. The bad ones were soon subjected to boos and hisses.

The Baptist Hall practically touched the back of the main bus garage run by United Counties. Here there had been riotous scenes, fights and workers' demonstrations during the 1926 General Strike. To begin with, the depression did not hit the boot and shoe factories. But as differences between the bosses and the workers grew, relations were made worse by employers' attempts to break the Strike, sometimes by setting on unemployed workers and virtually locking out regular employees.

The transport workers, especially those at the Harborough Road garage, were on strike in 1926. The employers, however, were required to run at least one bus a day down the usual route from Harborough to Kettering. If they did not, they might lose their licence.

It was amazing how quickly it became known when a bus might try to drive through Desborough. A crowd gathered and lined the pavement outside the garage and opposite below Riley's Boot and Shoe factory. Sometimes Grandad would let me watch from the window, where he worked at Riley's. I could see everything from there. The police, drafted in to keep the peace, lined the route but stood little chance of holding back the fierce opposition to the strike-breakers. As the bus came through at top speed, the driver was met by cries of 'Scab!' and a hail of stones was thrown at the bus.

There was no doubt whose side most of Desborough was on. Although the Strike began to peter out and strikers go back to work, it took many years to restore good relations in the transport industry.

By the time I started Grammar School in 1929, everything seemed back to normal. The bus companies were still running double-deckers with open tops and steps to climb to go upstairs, outside the seating areas. The Company had not yet thought of introducing single-decker buses, with entrances near the driver and he given the job of collecting fares as well as driving. Conductors were expected to climb the stairs every time a new passenger opted to go upstairs, rather than into the crowded lower deck.

Luckily, conductors always seemed to be likeable characters. Our favourite conductor made a practice of greeting everybody as they got on with:

'No rain, brothers! Not a drop! Ain't it luverly?'

If it did happen to be raining, he would get out, hold his hand out and announce:

'Only a few spots! It'll stop anytime now!'

These greetings were always followed by him grasping the cord connected to the driver's bell and shouting:

'Hold very tight, brothers. We're off!'

He would then swiftly pull the bell-cord and expect everybody who was standing to grab one of the supports hanging from the roof.

This particular conductor – an expert on all the latest football and cricket scores amongst a vast range of other knowledge – would keep the whole bus happy throughout the journey and get off to guide elderly passengers on their way, if they were in fear of getting lost.

Such people helped others to face difficult times by making them smile. They were real 'characters'.

Father's Family

I had a lot of relatives living in Rowell, 2 miles away, mostly my father's brothers and sisters. There had been 13 of them, but some of them died young, a frequent occurrence in large families at that time. My father had been killed in France, one of the thousands who fell near Ypres in March 1918. The Germans launched their final onslaught on British lives there at the end of the Great War, before the allies combined to push them back. The Germans sued for an Armistice in November 1918. Another younger brother, Ernest, was discharged from the Army that year, having been badly gassed and left mortally wounded. Other brothers were not accepted as fit to serve, mainly because of poor eyesight. They were, however, producing much needed Army boots.

All this I learned later. I had been born in Desborough 3 months before my father was killed. It is unlikely that Mother took me to Rowell to visit the Woolston family, particularly after she got the news of Father's death. At that time, there was no public transport, no buses or trains going to Rowell. She would have had to rely on horse-drawn carts or walk with the pram, 2 hard miles there and back. Sometimes, the daughters came down to see me, but that was all the contact we had, at least until I started school at 4. As a result, Father's family were not well known to me nor I to them.

As I grew older, invitations came to us to join their special celebrations, Christmas and Rowell Fair at Whitsuntide. Inevitably, there was a certain coolness between them and us, at least to begin with. To their minds, it seemed that Mother had taken a son of theirs two miles away and had made the new home there, at Desborough. Father had still worked, however, at the Avalon, a Co-op boot and shoe factory in Rowell, and no doubt went to his family's home nearby for dinner, with his brothers and sisters. All the same, it was as if Mother had caused a rift not easy to bridge.

The Woolston family was founded around Samuel, the jolly, plump, patriarchal head of the family, always placed at the head of the table, in his armchair and near the range on which meals had to be prepared. He had been a trade union organizer in the boot and shoe trade and was known to, and socialized happily with, everybody. We children noted that he was always served his meals first – it was the usual custom that the head of the family was treated thus – and got the pick of everything. Principal workers in any family had to be looked after by their wives. Grandma Woolston seemed to us a strange partner for one so good-humoured. She had the colouring and the appearance of a gipsy. Her jet-black hair was tied tightly to her head and plaited at the back. The end of the pigtail was marked with a dark bow. If the hair had to be tidier, she would fix it with hair-pins round the top of her head, round and round as far as it would go. She had a shrill voice and, in fierce tones, would call any child to order, who did not stay quiet and behave properly. As Sam cut the substantial leg of beef for this special occasion, Grandma put the best pieces on Sam's plate with a mixture of vegetables and kept it hot, whilst the rest of us were served. If it was a Sunday or Christmas Day, there would always be a separate Yorkshire pudding and gravy, served before the meat. We were expected to have a good appetite, but to eat everything up we were given, all the fat included.

The daughters were not good eaters like my brother Arthur and me. Clara, the eldest, was pale and slightly blue in complexion, maybe having a heart problem. She never looked keen to eat. Hilda, the next oldest, was dark-haired, smiled at us, occasionally, and even helped us to food we would not otherwise have dared to take. Mabel was smaller, another sickly girl, who, sadly, died young. Maud, the youngest, was the one we liked best. She was always game for a bit of fun, and usually took us out of harm's way, as soon as the meal was over.

She was a great believer in everybody having a good time, especially at Christmas. She would persuade Grandad Woolston to give her money to buy the kind of things everybody expected at Christmas – a Christmas tree, of course, and all kinds of decorations to go with it, festive fruits and lots of mysterious, but brightly-coloured parcels. On Christmas Eve, we had to hang up large stockings at the foot of the bed (Aunt Maud said 'Maybe a pillow-case if you can find an empty one!') and be ready to welcome Father Christmas that night. We had not to forget he would come after a long journey, climb down the chimney and expect to find some food there.

Christmas is coming, the goose is getting fat
Please put a penny in the old man's hat
If you haven't got a penny, a ha'penny will do
If you haven't got a ha'penny, then God bless you!

Like all excited children, we woke up before it was light and looked around. Sure enough, there were the stockings, bulging with all kinds of surprises, and more toys wrapped up on the bed. We took hold of our stockings first (long and large, lent by Aunt Maud) and found an orange, an apple, some dates and nuts, but right down the toe of the stocking, a mysterious, heavily wrapped package. After stripping off layer after layer of the wrapping, we found not a special titbit from Santa, but a small piece of coal, with instructions not to break our teeth on it! Just the start of fun and games at Christmas, inspired by Aunt Maud.

Most of Father's family, now grown up and married, lived in that same street,

Ragsdale Street. It had been named after a local benefactor, who had left money to provide a row of almshouses for the poor of Rowell. It gave a feeling of superiority to those who lived in Ragsdale Street, nearly all in their own houses.

Grandad Woolston's house was double-fronted, with bay windows either side of the central front door. At the side of the house, an entry covered by rooms above and protected by a substantial gate to keep out intruders. We did notice that Aunt Maud and her boyfriend, Cyril, lingered there a long time, before Cyril left for home, several miles away. Round the back corner of the house was a long pantry, leading to a back entrance and entrance hall. The pantry was to the right and the living room ahead and to the left. Further round the large window of the living room was another entrance and long, well-stocked workshops full of tools and lasts for shoe making and repairs. Further on still into the back garden was a hen-run, with boxes in the coop behind and lids we could lift up and take out the hen's eggs. There was plenty of wire netting to keep the hens in. Some fine-looking cocks were there as a protection to the ladies.

'Come and look at all these hens.' called out Aunt Maud to us. 'Those white ones are White Leghorns and the red ones next door Rhode Island Reds. Really healthy and good layers. You can tell that by how red their combs are.'

We rapidly absorbed this new information.

'You mustn't open the gate and let them out or they'll be off next door, looking for more worms.'

'That cock looks a bit scary!' was Arthur's opinion, but we soon found we could scare him off with a pretence of rushing to attack him. That caused some noise and flurry.

It was time to turn back and explore higher up the street. Aunt Maud introduced us first to Uncle Jack, her eldest brother. He, too, was sitting in an armchair, much as Grandfather Woolston did, and listening to the wireless.

'Come on in, boys, and sit you down. Now tell me about yourselves. Both at school now?'

We told him whose class we were in. He told us about his two boys. Leslie, his youngest, was in a comparable class to me. Later, he would join me at the Kettering Grammar School.

'Percy will be back soon. He's going to be a teacher, you know.'

We did not respond. The news was presented as an achievement for Percy. He would not be working in a local factory like most of his contemporaries.

'Maybe, they would like some tea. There should be some cake left, too?'

The question was addressed to Aunt Maud, but she excused us on the grounds that we had to call on Uncle Ernie and Aunt Millie, just along the top road.

They were some of our favourite relatives, who always made a great fuss of us and helped us build garages, railway stations and lines all over the large living room floor. There was, for Arthur and me, a great sense of space and freedom.

It was usual in those days for families, as they grew, to aim to find a house, as far as possible, in the same street as the parents. That way they could always offer help to those in need of it, especially during times of illness. There were two exceptions to this custom in the Woolston family – the twins, known always as Poll and Em, both 6 feet tall and married with families of their own. Arthur and I were quite surprised to meet grown-up twins. Those we knew in Desborough were always our age. It would certainly be a new experience to meet these older twins, who lived in Crispin Street, at the bottom end of Rowell, near the cemetery in Kettering Road. Their husbands worked in factories down there. Poll was married to Uncle Ben, a plump and jolly man, also given to sitting in his armchair, but smoking a pipe, which he removed briefly to say 'Hello!' to the two of us.

To us, he looked old, like everybody we knew who was approaching that vast age of 40. But, happily, he had a fund of stories to tell us boys, often about the tricks he used to get up to when he was young. No doubt Aunt Poll didn't really approve of Ben talking to us about Tricks and Treats he used to play on the neighbours. Uncle Ben always seemed to have lots of time to give to entertaining us. I can still hear his chuckle as he came to the end of a story. He didn't talk much about work in the factory, but instead took us out the back to see his 'shop' where he repaired family and neighbours' shoes. He showed us the trick we had seen Uncle Harry, the shoe mender, play in his 'shop'. These skilled workers with shoes used to fill their mouth with tacks as they hammered lots of them into a new sole being fitted to a shoe in for repair. The tacks were, apparently, tucked in a pouch in the corner of the mouth and taken out easily and without dropping any, to use at great speed. The amazing part was that both Uncle Harry and Uncle Ben could carry on a conversation at the same time with visitors to their 'shop' and never swallow one tack!

Poll had one daughter only, Eva, a year older than me, but happy, at a moment's notice, to take us out to the green lane at the back of the garden. There we could play and fantasiZe for hours, without adult interruption. When it was time to go, Eva bade me a sad good-bye. Obviously, I had made a lasting impression on her.

'Oh, Trevor, if only you lived a bit closer! We could have such fun!'

It was a plea she repeated later in life, even when I had left Northamptonshire for good. A sad parting of ways for both of us.

We were always expected to call on the other twin, Em, whenever we visited Poll. Em made us welcome, too, but she had a large family to look after, boys older than me, with the eldest already working in a factory. Girls, too, three at that time, tall like their mother and seeming to look down on us little ones. They were expected to help their mother with the vast amount of domestic chores Em seemed to be continuously involved in. It was washing all the time, each and every day, spread around the house to dry. Em's house always had that special smell of damp washing. She really had so many intensive commitments that it was impossible for her to ask us to stay.

In any case, we preferred to spend more time with Eva over the way. The relationship was later strengthened when she, too, won a scholarship to the High School, the school for girls attached to the Grammar School. Arthur was already there and somehow, was being paid for. Eva went a year before me. We three would face life together.

When I reflect now on those exploratory trips to Rowell relatives, the background to these new-found friends is of gardens close to every house. I recall the first crops showing through in the spring, peas and broad beans, runner beans outstripping those nearer the ground as they climb up two rows of supporting sticks. Later in the year, rows of cabbages, cauliflowers and broccoli, followed by the crowning glory, apples.

I got a great sense of satisfaction in how much there was in common with our Desborough house and the allotments Grandad Dawkins took me to. It gave everybody and surely particularly the children, the fact that life was solid and dependable and would go on like that for ever. After all, the Great War was the War to end all Wars!

Rowell Fair

Every year, around Whitsuntide, a fair was held in Rowell. It was a big fair and a thriving market for farmers from miles around. There was plenty of space too, right down the whole length of the town centre. In the middle of it all, a very impressive stone building, the Market Hall.

Before 6 a. m. on the Monday of Fair Week, the farmers brought in animals they wanted to sell, driving them along every road converging on the town centre. The farmers and their dogs followed on foot, driving their animals just as fast as they would go, using ash sticks. From the entry to the market place and lining the edges of both sides, up against the pavement, were cattle, horses, sheep, pigs and poultry. A few goats, too, to lend some dignity to the occasion.

Precisely, at 6 o'clock, when the church clock struck, the Town Crier appeared in his full regalia, swinging his precious bell and shouting 'Oyez, oyez!' He stopped at various points of the market place to announce, reading from an ancient scroll, that a market would open that day, and naming the animals which would be on show. Naturally, he had a great following of children, full of excitement, cheering wildly whenever he concluded his proclamation and finally stopped to talk to his friends. Somehow, they were able to get beer from the many pubs, even at that hour. The Town Crier and his circle were soon in merry frame of mind, encouraging everybody to enjoy themselves.

The children my brother and I were with had a swift look round the various stalls being erected. There was everything from dolls to shooting ranges, Aunt Sallies and coconut stalls, our special delight. Four balls for 6d to try to knock down a coconut, but not yet. We noted with pleasure the roundabout had come again, with its organ, round which galloping horses would rotate and take their riders dangerously up and down, where they were suspended. Careful parents sat smaller children on first and then got on the horse to hold them tight. That, too, would get going later. In later years – nobody seemed to know when this part of the fair developed – a new form of excitement was introduced, no doubt designed to match the motor-cars beginning to appear, the Dodgems. These small cars holding two children in each, looked rather like motor-cars, but they depended on electricity to propel them round and a driving wheel to control the direction the Dodgem would be driven. The aim was, usually, to bump other cars, but, if possible, to avoid getting bumped yourself. There were slides, too, which seemed highly dangerous when setting off from the top. Needless to say, sophisticated children swiftly learned how to slide down on a mat head-first or to link up with a mate. Accidents were very rare. Maybe, somebody got bumped at the bottom and ended up in a heap with his successor on top of him.

After that swift look round, we ran home for breakfast. The food was always good and plentiful during Fair Week, so we had a good breakfast to set us up for the day. For later meals, dinner or tea, every family bought what was known as Rowell Fair ham, a huge joint, which could be cut into for the rest of the week. But, after breakfast, we ran back again to see if the rest of the fair had been set up. The auction of animals for sale was going on meantime.

The day we looked forward to was when Uncle Cyril, the boyfriend of Aunt Maud, had a half-day's holiday. Uncle Cyril was an engine driver, clearly a man of some importance. He was also very tall and could throw coconut balls like bullets. Whereas we could sometimes hit one of the coconuts (usually placed in a cup on top of a strong stick) without dislodging it, Uncle Cyril could knock down at least two with four balls. Occasionally, more. These would be given to Arthur and me. We would carry them with great pride. After all, coconuts in those days really looked like coconuts. A hard, hairy shell, which had to be cracked to sample the inner skin of coconut, and a tufty end, which it could be held by. We also liked to knock nails into soft spots on the opposite end to the tuft and drain out the milk, which was tasty and sweet. A whole coconut would last a long time, but if we ate it quickly, Uncle Cyril would always get us some more. Both he and Aunt Maud took us to the fair and paid for us to sample some of the sideshows. Being out with adults meant also that we could stay out late.

Rowell Fair week never lasted long enough for us children. We took every opportunity to make it last longer, even making friends with Uncle Walter, when Uncle Cyril was away working. Walter was the youngest of the Woolstons, with a reputation for being a bit on the mean side. Maybe it would be kinder to say his attitude to money was that he was just being careful. He did make Arthur and me welcome if we went to see him just above the family house but down an entry on the opposite side of the street. He showed us his garden and what was growing there and his carefully arranged workshop near the back door. His wife, Doll, was totally different in temperament and behaviour. A real red-head with a reputation for being ready with a quick response to something said which didn't suit her. Her whole life at that moment was given over to looking after a new baby, Audrey, who, after going through the elaborate ritual of changing her nappy, being bathed and powdered and decked out in clean, new clothes (all a novel and interesting process for Arthur and me) was put out in her pram to entertain us until she got sleepy. Audrey was their only child, as it turned out, but it was noticeable that it was wholly Doll's business to see she had everything she needed. Doll would then go into the kitchen to prepare meals. Again, we noticed that she was in no hurry to be tied down to household duties. She liked to go across to have a chat with the rest of the family and with neighbours too, if they were around.

Walter rather gloomily waited and in case we were holding things up, suggested we went back and had our tea and he would take us to the fair later on. It was a suggestion we were glad to take up. In due course, we latched on to Uncle Walter as he strolled rather leisurely down to the fair.

We noticed it was not the same as when we went with Uncle Cyril and Aunt Maud. It was much more a case of watching other people trying to knock off a coconut or going down the slide, rather than being given money to have a go ourselves. Uncle Walter apparently recognized that he could not compete with Uncle Cyril in throwing four balls for 6d, so he stood back and didn't even try. It was all very proper and well-behaved, as far as Arthur and I were concerned, but just a bit of a disappointment all the same. I guess we dragged our heels on the return journey to Ragsdale Street, but, as instructed by Mother, thanked Uncle Walter for taking us to the fair and disappeared quickly indoors.

There was always a cricket match on Rowell Fair Monday. It was the local Derby between Desborough and Rowell, and Uncle Ben said he would take us. He would be able to tell us about all the well-known players – the match-winners – on both sides, whom he knew. For Rowell, Jackie Willis was their great hero. A left-arm bowler round the wicket, who threw the ball in the air, so that it would drop shorter than the batsman expected and if it landed in front of him, it would spin away, perhaps just touching the bat and being caught by the wicket-keeper. To avoid getting trapped this way, a batsman would sometimes run down the pitch, aiming to hit the ball for a boundary, before it bounced. The chances then were that the ball dropped too soon to be hit. The batsmen would miss it and be stumped. It was certainly an art and a matter of great excitement to us boys, trying not to show we favoured Desborough to win.

There was a break for tea, with honours even. One of the Desborough batsmen knew how to deal with the left-hand wizard and had continued to add runs without being out at tea-time. Uncle Ben took us to the pavilion for an ice-cream and we were allowed to sample roast chestnuts from another stall, a new experience for both of us. Another boy there had even found a toffee apple, which might have been more to my liking.

Play resumed after tea, and after adding a few more swiftly made runs, Desborough declared and Rowell had to try to pass a formidable score.

Wickets began to fall to the Desborough fast bowlers and everybody was on edge to see whether they could win the match. In the last few overs, Rowell were still holding out with two wickets to fall. Then another batsman was out, but the last pair defended to the end. A draw, they said, and proceeded to analyse the good and bad features of the match. Uncle Ben chewed it over with Rowell supporters who found lots of reasons why they should have won. To begin with, the batsman who made all the runs for Desborough should have been given out in his first over. The Desborough umpire had disallowed an appeal for a catch behind the wicket. Rowell had been robbed!

Arthur and I could make little sense of it all, but we knew we had had a good day with Uncle Ben and learned a lot from him. He promised to take us again. After that, Rowell Fair was soon over for another year. We had Desborough Feast to look forward to in September in the Rec. Celebrations then were concentrated on the evening activities. Bright lights, the noise of the fair and lots of stalls selling tit-bits and cheap ornaments. No Town Crier, no 6 a. m. start. It really hadn't the same attractions as we had enjoyed at Rowell. Perhaps I should take Eva's advice and go and live near her.

But Mam wouldn't like that, nor Grandma and Grandad. I would miss them, too ... No, it would be better to keep Rowell Fair as that really exciting week which we would spend with my Dad's relations and of course, the Fair.

Guy Fawkes

The preparation for Guy Fawkes Night on 5 November used to be something special. He was a real person to us children. Not exactly a villain whose image we were aiming to destroy. Rather a friend of ours, who could take on all kinds of appearances depending on what we could find to construct this strange figure, who would eventually be placed on the top of the bonfire and be burnt. Each of us would collect what we thought would make part of his body. An old pair of trousers for his bottom half. Padded sticks to form the bones of his legs. If we were lucky, an old pair of boots to fill as his feet. Similarly, someone would find an old jacket, maybe a threadbare pullover, from which we could make his chest and arms. Arms could be finished off with a stuffed pair of gloves. One of the more artistic members of our gang would be given the job of constructing his head. It was important to complete the head with an amusing, rather friendly, face – probably a rounded piece of brown cardboard tied to a filled ball or pig's bladder and coloured in with eyes, ears, mouth and hair. No need for a great deal of hair. One of Grandad's old hats could finish off the top of the head. Maybe a coloured feather stuck in at the side, just to show how lively he was.

We would work on this almost-living doll for days and finally put him in a wheelbarrow to take round the village crying 'Penny for the Guy! Penny for the Guy!' and

'Please to remember
The fifth of November
Gunpowder, treason and plot
We know no reason
Why gunpowder treason
Should ever be forgot.'

We were lucky to have enough money to buy sparklers (lit with a match and shooting out sparks from a thick wire stick) and maybe that fireworks wonder, a Catherine Wheel pinned to a post. Nowadays, there is little artistry in Bonfire Night. People seem to have forgotten what is its significance. Lots of bangers and rockets are used to promote a kind of phoney excitement, almost throughout the year.

Guy Fawkes was very real to us. He had made his preparations to blow up

Parliament just down the road. His Catholic friends gathered at Rushton Lodge, where the Treshams lived. At the corner of the estate, tucked in behind a wall was this ancient monument known as the Triangular Lodge. Everything about it had been built triangular in shape, probably of religious significance. It had several storeys and stairs inside mounted its three sides, with little slits in the corners of the walls, clearly designed for defensive purposes, should any Cromwellian supporters decide to attack those defending the Lodge.

It was an amazing building and when we were children we could quietly climb in and explore. Since then, it has become more like a museum. First, an ancient monument and now, looked after by English Heritage. You now have to pay to go in. Children's imagination can no longer make it an exciting place to explore in and play Civil War games.

There are many other stories of those times that have been uncovered. The remains of a Catholic Abbey are to be found some two miles away at Rowell and some evidence has been found of a tunnel being built between that Abbey and Rushton Hall, so that Guy Fawkes supporters could disappear underground when attacked and go to whichever place, Rushton or Rowell, might offer temporary shelter.

We used to look for traces of this tunnel, when we walked between a farm, known as Harry Cook's, near the Triangular Lodge, and Rowell. There was a footpath over those fields. If we had not become obsessed with playing in the old sandstone hay-barn of Harry Cook's, trying to operate the turnip cutting machine, hiding in the hay-carts or the hay-loft, we would set out over a stile nearby, walk down to the Ise Brook, climb the triangular wooden construction which enabled us to get over the water collecting there in flood times, and make for Rowell up the hill on the other side. This path ended in the allotments to the south of Rowell. These again, could absorb our interest, but usually, we would give up the plan to make for the Abbey and divert into Father's parental home and maybe get some tea offered by my aunts.

If it was nearly Guy Fawkes time, we would not stay. There were no boys around making preparations for 5 November no searching of bottom cupboards to help clothe him. Just the routine feeding of the hens in the back garden. Nothing exciting, so we would set off back to Desborough, through the Market Place and up past the old Abbey. It was all much the same as we had seen before and parts of it had even been fenced round and locked up. So we would take the hill back to the Ise Brook bridge, cross over and take the short cut home over the fields and past the church. No link with Guy Fawkes there, but maybe behind the high wall on the opposite side to the church school, some preparations were going on. The church boys, even though they might be rivals of ours, had every intention of celebrating 5 November and were collecting wood and rubbish where they could. No sign of a Guy being made, however. At least we were a few steps ahead of them.

The thought was enough to make us smarten our pace and get back to finish off our Guy. He was, of course, the best that would be made in either Desborough or Rowell. We were the greatest! Or were we, sad to say, beginning to prepare the way for football fans chanting the supremacy of their team? Rivalry seemed much more friendly and easy-going in those days.

On 5 November, everything was brought out from various corners where things had been hidden and the special area prepared for our Guy. First, we cleared our usual spot in the back garden up near Cyril Draper's. There was a reasonable area of sky showing there, where trees would not be burnt by the bonfire. There were some vulnerable pear trees there and a Coster apple on the other side.

We began to lay the foundations of the fire, supervised by Grandad, lots of dry wood, paper and cardboard at the bottom to get the fire going. On the assumption that everything would go according to plan, we piled plenty of combustible material high and crowned it all with Guy, looking happy and pleased at being the central attraction.

The children in houses around came in and joined us, bringing small contributions of their own and all of us being careful to put any fireworks in boxes well clear of the flames. As soon as it was dark, Grandad put a light to the area specially prepared to get the bonfire really going. We all stood back anxiously awaiting the result. It was always a bit uncertain to begin with, especially if, as often happened, it came on to rain. But, generally speaking, there would be quite a sudden flare-up and in no time, the heat was almost unbearable. Guy looked surprised and not too happy about this strange deception. Not the kind of end to the occasion he had been expecting. We added more fuel and Guy's clothes took light. We all became anxious for his future, his makers most of all. There was no stopping now. He was alight and about to perish. A mixture of cheers and groans confirmed his sad end. The children tried to get closer to see whether he was still there. One small child departed, crying, carried by her mother. She had been hurt by a flying spark. Other children tried to get hold of sticks from the fire and drag them away still burning. There was no more to burn, but the embers would glow in the dark for hours yet.

There was nothing for it but to leave this scene of imaginary carnage. Parents gathered the small children up and carried them out. Bigger boys did their best to make it last longer, but soon were saying good-night to their friends and regretting that it would be another year before 5 November came round again.

Arthur and I went to see what remained next morning. A huge heap of ash and what appeared to be one of Guy Fawkes' arms, sticking out above. It looked like a hand with glove attached, as though he had fought to the end to get out of that hell-fire, and was almost cocking a snook at his tormentors. Maybe he meant 'So you thought you would get rid of me? Don't worry, I'll be back next year!'

Grandad Dawkins Begins a New Life

Grandad retired from Riley's Boot and Shoe Factory when he reached the age of 65. That, I realized, meant big changes for him and the rest of us. Grandad was well-liked and had earned the respect of his workmates. He would, undoubtedly, miss their company. He was given a good send-off. Everybody who had worked with him – indeed, the whole factory – clubbed together to buy him a silver watch, duly inscribed inside. Grandad treasured this watch, which he always kept in the fob-pocket of his waistcoat. We used to watch him pull the watch out, snap open the cover and check the time, repeatedly, through the day. It became a natural part of his everyday behaviour, his link with the past, but now a pointer to a new life.

There was no doubt his release, from a regime of rigid hours and concentration on his work as a clicker, made him a new man. He was now able to indulge in all those special interests acquired over the years. Because he was very deaf, an affliction from scarlet fever as a child, he loved to read all kinds of books. He had a built-in glass-fronted bookcase, packed with books, old and new. At the bottom, an early edition of Encyclopaedia Britannica, with some of his favourite reading books just above and his diaries, in which he made careful entries daily. Arthur and I were allowed space above for our Sunday School prizes, along with family photograph albums, which we all treasured. Grandma claimed the drawers below, where she kept her glasses, reels of cotton and needles. A large bottom cupboard contained clean sheets, pillow-cases and household items.

Grandad, seated in his favourite armchair, near the front bay window, listened a great deal to the wireless. In those early days, he first had a wooden HMV horn, which provided him with some amplification of sound. But, to get the best results, he held his right ear right inside this horn. He would search out the best BBC programmes, but rarely failed to listen on Sunday evenings. He had given up going to the Chapel because of his deafness, and now turned instead to the Service from St Martin's-in-the-Fields, followed by the Palm Court weekly concert from Eastbourne. Sunday was then a strictly non-working day, but a day of deep pleasure for Grandad.

Almost invariably, there is a great burst of energy with retirement from regular work, a return of youthful vigour and delight in physical activities. This very soon showed itself in Grandad. He had been a builder in his youth and developed his muscles lifting weights, climbing buildings and walking with his barrow around building sites. Although he was a small man, he was tough. Just to look at, he was neat and tidy, with black hair and a small moustache, a worker. His past experience was now applied to improving our large garden and orchard.

He first weighed up how this large space should be used. The paths had to be fit to support loaded barrows pushed to and fro, but, first, improvements had to be made, immediately outside the back of the house. In his initial enthusiasm for cramming in fruit trees of all kinds, he had set espalier pears almost into the house foundations. One pear tree was already too big, its roots pushing up the blue builder's tiles near the back door and making them dangerous to walk on. The path had to be re-laid and overgrown trees removed. Jimmy Burton, an even tougher young ironstone worker helped him.

Grandma wanted better access to and from 17 Queen Street, where Elsie, her eldest daughter lived. Grandad had the solution. When the house was first built, he had acquired a huge load of flat, blue bricks, ideal for making a path. The bricks were rectangular in shape, but narrower than red bricks used on the house, and longer. Grandad and Jimmy Burton set about laying a path to the top of the garden, right round the corner to Elsie's. It was very attractive and hard-wearing. It pleased Grandma also that her washing-line could be extended alongside the path.

That led, naturally, to the tidying-up of the top end of the garden. There had once been a pig-sty and hen-run here. Remnants were still standing, where Grandad kept his barrows and gardening tools. A glass greenhouse had proved to be badly placed alongside. Its glass panes were soon shattered by falling branches and heavy pears from the stewing pear tree. A zinc roof had then been mounted on wooden supports, where long ladders could be stored. Grandad had, no doubt, already planned to build a new greenhouse in an open area at the bottom of the garden. But that, when the top of the garden was being tidied up, was just a dream.

In case he had not set himself enough to do, Grandad decided to level the lawn, which extended most of the way from top to bottom of the garden. It was no easy task, with fruit trees of all kinds growing there and extending roots and branches everywhere. Even to make a start near the house was a tough undertaking. There were bumps and roots to be removed, hollows to be filled up. Grandad bought a new bright green wheelbarrow and a spade to remove unwanted bumps. He made a wooden stamper to smooth it all down and set grass-seed where turf had been removed. A heavy roller was needed to firm the whole area. Grandad had a solution to that. He obtained a large empty can, filled it with concrete, and, with the help of Frisby's, a Havelock Street firm who claimed they could solve any farming or gardening problem, had a central axle and T-shaped handle made of iron, fixed to the roller. Quite an invention and heavy enough to compress any stretch of soil.

When the lawn was finally completed, Arthur and I were delighted to find an area set aside further over, which we could use as a cricket pitch. But, the grass had to be cut, regularly, and Grandad went off on a search for a suitable lawnmower. The one he favoured was bought, second-hand, from Alf Ball, the blacksmith. Grandad must have been attracted by its unusual mechanism. It had a large metal roller at the back, to which a chain was attached to turn the cutting knives at the front. An additional wooden roller at the front could be raised and lowered to vary the cutting distance from the ground. The main problem with this lawnmower was that it was heavy to push. Arthur and I had to tie a rope to the front, to help Grandad get it uphill.

It did seem an inclination of Grandad to acquire unusual tools, which were often too heavy for him alone. The one which Grandma and Mother thoroughly disapproved of was Grandad's huge square truck. A very large box, in effect, made of thick, heavy planks, and mounted on heavy iron wheels, supported at the back by upright feet and heavy handle. Grandad tried to make lifting the truck easier by wearing a kind of harness over his shoulders. By the time several long ladders had been tied together on top and we set off for the Copeland allotment, down by the cemetery, extra help was needed. Coming back with a load of apples was even worse. Someone had to push the truck by the ladders, whilst someone else pulled in front and warned traffic coming from the opposite direction. It was much too heavy for Grandad, even with assistance, but he steadily maintained he needed such a big truck. After all, he had no horse and cart.

The truck was much too big to use in the orchard at home. Because there were some very tall trees, usually pear trees, two long ladders had to be tied together to reach the top branches. One of us stood at the foot of the heaviest ladder and pulled to raise it, whilst someone else pushed from underneath. After we had got the ladders upright, they had to be manoeuvred into a safe resting place. It was up to Grandad to achieve this. Even then, Arthur and I might climb the ladders and go still higher by hanging on to the top branches, making sure they really would hold us.

At more relaxed times, Grandad would ask us how we were getting on at school. In 1928, when Grandad retired, Arthur was at Kettering Grammar School. It would be another year before I took the scholarship exam. Arthur (lucky lad!) got much longer holidays than I did. Perhaps as part of his education, Grandad took him on trips to cities I had yet to discover. Rail travel was then very cheap. A special return ticket to London cost only 5/9d. Arthur was taken on visits to Central London – the Thames Embankment, Westminster Abbey, the Houses of Parliament, Big Ben, Tower Bridge and the Tower of London, Hyde Park and Buckingham Palace, Whitehall, the Cenotaph, Trafalgar Square, Nelson's Column and the National Gallery alongside. Goodness knows how they managed to visit all these places, but there was very little tourism then, plenty of red buses and room to move.

On another occasion, they visited Madame Tussaud's to gaze in wonder at the likenesses of Charlie Chaplin, Lloyd George and Henry VIII. The Empire Stadium, said to hold 100,000 people, was even more impressive. Its various pavilions were designed to show off the glories of our colonies. The Taj Mahal replica, one of the Seven Wonders of the World, was thought to be the showpiece by visitors. Grandad, occasionally, enquired, when Arthur and I were talking to him at home, what we would like to be when we grew up. Arthur wasn't sure. Maybe a teacher. I had no hesitation in saying I wanted to be a famous violinist like Albert Sammons. The family all took it for granted that we would not go into a factory. Grandad, no doubt, wondered, privately, whether Arthur might become a pharmacist like his Uncle Arthur.

So that I did not miss out on all these visits, Grandad and Uncle Harry took me on the train to Leicester, 20 miles away. The County Agricultural Show was held in Abbey Park along with the County Flower Show, but a more modest place to visit was the museum, quite near the station. There, I was amazed, and maybe a little appalled, by a portrait of Daniel Lambert, the heaviest man, at 26 stones, to have lived in Leicester. Alongside, there was his huge wooden armchair, at least a yard wide and just enough space to accommodate his huge thighs.

Uncle Harry was particularly keen on going to the centre of the city, near its four-faced clock tower, where there was a huge Market Hall. The main market stalls, selling vegetables and fruit, were in an open space. The Hall sheltered live rabbits and poultry in cages. We were greeted by salesmen shouting their special offers, ever willing to knock down the price, if necessary. We could hardly take live rabbits back to Desborough. This treasure of a place had to be left for local people.

Instead, Uncle Harry lured us to the noise and excitement of Leicester City Football Ground. We soon learned how different and skilled were the games played there, compared with our attempts at ball control back home in the Rec.

To match those Leicester visits, Arthur travelled to Birmingham, a city I knew nothing about. But Arthur proudly informed me that our ancestors, Dawkins, the Desborough builders, had built the Town Hall there, in the middle of the 19th century. He clearly regarded this as a mark of the family status. Curiously, much later, I came across a reproduction of Grandad's favourite picture, which hung for many years on the living room wall at 4 Regent Street. It was featured in The Times, as one of the art treasures hanging in Birmingham Art Gallery. It had also been there since about 1850 and was identical to Grandad's picture, except in one respect. The print was of 'The Choir Practice' and showed a violinist conducting a band of instrumentalists, cello and viola to the front of the picture and a big bass on the other side. A choir composed of singers of markedly different ages, stood together behind a table opposite the conductor and singing from sheet music. Both Grandad's picture and that in the Birmingham Art Gallery were coloured in sepia. The only difference was that the Art Gallery version showed the conductor wearing spectacles. Grandad's picture of the conductor had none. It made me wonder if Grandad's version was the original, but when I wrote to the Art Gallery for an explanation, they could offer none.

That, no doubt, was a side-track from Grandad giving it pride of place at home. To me, as I grew up a musician, it showed where Grandad's deepest affections lay. To him, all the instruments and the singers were familiar. He had been the church organist and later, a competent cellist. Music, clearly, meant a great deal to him. His picture left me with a deep feeling of gratitude that he passed his special interest on to me. Every step I took along the musical road, Grandad followed with delight and encouraged me to go further. Even when I left home for London and began to sever some of the family links, Grandad wanted to know more about the contacts I was making with the College of Violinists and who was teaching me. Such support helped a great deal in fostering the talent I held most dear. Music would stay with me forever.

Postlude

It is time I stopped. I'm afraid, Jodie, I have wandered into the realms of Erewhon, into an ancient fairyland you have not experienced.

The aim in all these stories of my childhood has been to find links with the past – exciting links at the time – which you, at the moment, know nothing about. Above all, I have tried to convey the importance of music in a young boy's life. Not all music, but that silver thread that came down to me from composers like Bach, Haydn, Mozart and Beethoven. It is a precious thread that you may find in more modern composers, like Bartok. The depth of feeling given to me by these men has reached the heart and shaped my life.

Why not yours, Jodie? It will give you immense pleasure and I shall feel proud that you have inherited that same passion.

I wonder if somebody, close to both of us, will say 'She got her musical talent from her great-grandfather!' To which, I might well retort 'But her personality and good looks from mum and dad!'

Wachet Auf

J. S. BACH